Sweet, Savage Death marks the first appearnce of tall, gangly, virtuous Patience McKenna, who writes romance novels for money and serious non-fiction for love, and whose subsequent detections will bring her into behind-the-scenes contact with some of the less publicized areas of publishing.

"A sophisticated and often amusing romp."

The New York Times Book Review.

JANE HADDAM

WRITING AS ORANIA PAPAZOGLOU

Sweet, Savage Death

INTERNATIONAL POLYGONICS , LTD.
NEW YORK CITY

Sweet, Savage Death

For my parents

For support moral, emotional,
and sometimes financial

For my brother, Xenophon

And my sister-in-law, Joan

And for Andrea, Jeremy, and Nicholas

Long may they wave

Sweet, Savage Death

FIRES OF LOVE
General Editorial Guidelines

Dear Romance Writer:

FARRET PAPERBACK ORIGINALS is proud to introduce a new concept in romance fiction, FIRES OF LOVE. Aimed at the contemporary woman who wants more romance, more passion, more sensual detail than can be found in traditional romance lines, FIRES OF LOVE will present realistic characters in provocative situations that mirror the problems and possibilities of women's lives today. To write for FIRES OF LOVE, you must have the passion and the insight to explore *all* facets of modern love and yet must be committed to the wonderful fantasy that is romance. Our stories will be sophisticated but not negative, sensual but not clinical. Most of all, they should be fun for the reader to read and for you, the writer, to write.

Please study the following guidelines carefully before submitting your manuscript to us; they're the very essence of FIRES OF LOVE:

The Heroine. Older than the traditional romance heroine (25 to 35), the central character of a FIRES OF LOVE novel is a feisty, modern, caring young woman with a stake in her world. We're looking for heroines with work they're deeply involved in, or at least an overwhelming outside interest. A FIRES OF LOVE heroine doesn't cry at the first sign of trouble or blush at a mere innuendo. She meets life head on. Although she has her faults, they're not serious; and on the whole, she exhibits a maturity beyond her years. She's got a sense of humor and the precious ability to laugh at herself, but she knows when to take herself seriously too. She's not a doormat and won't let the hero—or anyone else—turn her into one. Most importantly, a FIRES OF LOVE heroine must be an active participant in her love affair—and the directress of her life as well.

A FIRES OF LOVE heroine need not be a virgin, even if she has never been married. The subject may simply not come up. She takes a liberated, but not libertine, view of sexuality—knowing that it has its place in the love between a man and a woman. She is not, however, promiscuous. Rather she believes sex and love go together like a horse and carriage—and knows you need both to make a marriage! A FIRES OF LOVE heroine may be widowed or divorced. If divorced, however, it must be clear that the divorce was not her fault. In general, it is better if any previous relationship the heroine may have had pales in comparison to this new love.

The Hero. The hero is the man of every woman's dreams—if not rich, then spectacularly successful at what he does: handsome, caring, compassionate, and, of course, irresistibly sexy. He should be older than the heroine, ranging in age from 30 to 45, and well established in his career. We're looking here for the prototypical male: not a muscle-bound monstrosity, but an athletic, masculine dream. He should be strong-willed without being abusive, and should respect the heroine for her accomplishments as well as for her looks. Although he may have difficulty expressing his emotions, the FIRES OF LOVE hero feels deeply and strongly desires a commitment to a permanent relationship with the heroine.

The Setting. A FIRES OF LOVE romance can take place in the United States or abroad, in a crowded city or on a deserted desert island. Present the setting as romantically as possible—and use it to provide plot details and complications!

The Love Scenes. FIRES OF LOVE will present more frequent and explicit love scenes than are common in traditional romance, although a FIRES OF LOVE love scene should *never* be clinical. Rather, concentrate on what the heroine feels and thinks when she is making love to the hero. Tell us what is going on in her mind, how the rough touch of the hero's fingertips tease the rosy peaks of her breasts into frothy, pulsing sensors of desire; how the teasing challenge of the hero's tongue sends waves of passion to the very core of her being. Help us to experience this greatest of all fulfillments *with* the heroine—and remember that the focus of a FIRES OF LOVE love scene is on love, not passion alone.

The Plot. A FIRES OF LOVE plot concentrates on the growing relationship between the hero and the heroine. Remember that this is a fantasy. Heavy situations such as alcoholism, drug abuse, abortion, wife battering, inflation, chronic unemployment, and criminal activity are not appropriate here. There should be no elements of mystery or suspense, and no suggestions of the gothic. A FIRES OF LOVE novel is basically a story about a man and a woman and the ways they find each other. Your job is to create a story where true love conquers great odds —to end in marriage. Manuscripts should be approximately 60,000 words long.

Due to the recent proliferation of romance novels on the American publishing scene, a number of plot devices and conflicts have become, we feel, sadly overused. If possible, the FIRES OF LOVE author should avoid the following situations:

1. The heroine will not give in to the hero because she thinks he sleeps with too many other women, and doesn't believe in monogamous relationships.
2. The heroine will not give in to the hero because he thinks women do not belong in business or are not as competent as men.
3. The hero will not give in to the heroine because he thinks all women are promiscuous.
4. The hero will not give in to the heroine because he thinks she is a spoiled rich girl—which he disapproves of because he has had to work his way up from the bottom.

Since FIRES OF LOVE is a contemporary line, stories about arranged marriages or marriages of convenience are not acceptable.

The Style. A FIRES OF LOVE book should be written in the third person but from the heroine's point of view. Flashbacks should be kept to a minimum and flash forwards not used at all. Books should seem to exist outside time—as if they were happening today, no matter when today might be. For that reason, no references should be made to any event or dates that would fix the story in time—the Korean or Vietnam wars, for example. A FIRES OF LOVE novel should give the impression of taking place anytime and *everytime*.

Concentrate on sensual detail. The hero and heroine should be described often and at length, with frequent references to the clothes, food, and decorations involved in any fictional scene. Put the reader into the world of your novel. Let her feel, taste, smell, see, and hear your world!

We hope you're as excited about FIRES OF LOVE as we are—and we look forward to seeing your manuscript.

Good luck and good writing!

Janine Williams
Editor in Chief
FIRES OF LOVE

CHAPTER 1

I had a friend once who thought you could find out anything you wanted to know about a person from the way she dressed—the weight of the fabric, the colors of the cloth, the cut of the styling. If he had seen me for the first and only time at Myrra Agenworth's funeral, he would have thought me one of those tall women who is afraid of being tall, a self-conscious stooper, a drudge. He would have been right about only one thing. At Myrra's funeral, I was more self-conscious than I had been anytime since the sixth grade. I am six feet and weigh a hundred and twenty-five pounds. I am tall and look taller. I stood in the back of the People's Nondenominational Church on West Thirty-fourth Street and Tenth Avenue in a little black-nothing dress fresh from the SFAntastic Collection at Saks, looking like a stork.

I had my hair, which is very thick and blonde and falls to my waist, tied into a braid. I was gripping the pew in front of me and trying not to faint. I was also trying not to laugh. A three-day bout of fasting, brought on by my inability to fit into a size-seven bathing suit I had tried on in Bloomingdale's for no other reason than that I had never seen anything so aggressively grotesque, had left me giddy and out of control.

The pastor raised his eyes to heaven and said, in the tone of a chipmunk spying an untended cache of nuts, "Dear Lord, take to your bosom this woman of love."

I put my head in my hands and peered through my fingers at the first three rows of pews, determined to concentrate on the sociology of the spectacle. It wasn't difficult.

Myrra Agenworth had died alone at the hand of a mugger in River-side Park at two-thirty on the morning of December second, while she was out walking her dog. What she was doing walking a cocker spaniel in Riverside Park at two-thirty in the morning was never satisfactorily determined. There was some feeling at the time that it didn't really matter. The woman was seventy-six years old, frail, eccentric at the best of times, rich beyond the point where her judgment could be readily questioned. If she wanted to walk out into the Manhattan night in diamond earrings, a ruby necklace that covered her breasts like a coat of mail, and a floor-length chinchilla cape, it was her business, and the doorman certainly wasn't going to stop her. What mattered was that she was alone. Her children were all dead. Her one granddaughter lived in England, had just graduated from Oxford, and spent as little time with her grandmother as possible. There was some friction there, but it was to be expected. The son of one of the other romance novelists I know tells his friends his mother takes in typing for a living—anything to avoid the embarrassment of being related to a woman who writes "those drippy love books."

Myrra had written her funeral service before her death, decided on the People's Nondenominational Church, and chosen the props. It was left to her publishers to find thirteen dozen roses, thirteen doves, a peacock, and a heart-shaped casket. They didn't manage the casket. They had to settle for an ordinary one, with a broken heart carved into the wood above the place where Myrra's head was supposed to be.

The service was carefully planned for December tenth, the Thursday before the Sunday that would open the Third Annual Conference of the American Writers of Romance. Every important romance novelist and editor in the country was due at the Cathay-Pierce Hotel on Friday. The editors at Farret Paperback Originals got them in on Thursday and packed the first three rows of pews with brand name authors from twenty-two states and three countries. Barbara Cartland came with a bit of black veiling pinned into her improbably bouffant hair. Rosemary Rogers managed to look grief-stricken. Even Bertrice Small held up her little square of pew, looking a trifle grim and a trifle sad and a trifle lost.

In the fourth row they placed the most important editors in category romance: Vivian Stephens of Harlequin, Karen Solem of Silhouette,

Anne Gisonny of Candlelight at Dell, Ellen Edwards and Leslie Kazan-
jian of Berkley/Jove, Carolyn Nichols of Bantam. Janine Williams of
Farret was there, in the center of the row, her little brown bun covered
with a black snood perched exactly two and one half inches above the
collar of her black suit jacket. Her back was straight, her shoulders were
squared, and her suit was a Harvé Bernard she shouldn't have tried to
afford. She looked expensively uncomfortable, but she also looked the
quintessential editor. For the moment that was even more important
than grief. CBS had a camera crew in the lobby.

"Chocolates," Phoebe whispered into my waist. "They're going to
pass out chocolates."

She sounded cheerful and disgusted at once—cheerful about the
prospect of one of those little heart-shaped, cream-filled chocolates
from Godiva, disgusted because Amelia Samson was passing them out.
Amelia Samson was what Phoebe called "one of the old school," as if
romance writing was an army making the transition from horse cavalry
to motorized tanks. Amelia was in her early sixties, somewhat over two
hundred pounds, and the "author" of over two hundred category
romances. She even had her own line, put out by Farret, called "Amelia
Samson's Lovelines." What Phoebe objected to was the fact that
Amelia Samson didn't actually do any writing, and hadn't for nearly
twenty years. She barricaded herself in a forty-room house in Rhine-
beck called "The Castle," surrounded herself with a dozen aging, fawn-
ing women, and fed each of them a detailed plot and character outline
every month. They wrote the novels. They accepted board and minimum wage.

Phoebe was six months younger than I was, four feet eleven inches
tall, one hundred thirty pounds, and *determined*. She was determined
on general principles, and it suited her. Needless to say, she wrote her
own books. She wrote very long books, almost never touched category
romance, and still managed to produce two paperback originals a year.
She had changed her last name from Weiss to Damereaux, wallpapered
her ten-room apartment in varying shades of velvet, and appeared in
the pages of *People* magazine wearing a floor-length scarlet velvet caftan, six strands of rope diamonds, pear-shaped diamond earrings so

heavy they made her earlobes droop, and no fewer than two amethyst rings on each of her eight fingers. The ex-wife of her insurance agent, who subscribed to *People*, sent a copy of the article to her ex-husband's front office. Six weeks later, after an extensive investigation involving dozens of pained-looking young men in brown linen suits, they canceled her theft, homeowner's, and life insurance policies.

"Not chocolates," Phoebe said sadly, "orchids."

Amelia stopped at our row and passed the basket, a mock Tyrolean affair with red and white ribbons wound around the handles. When it reached me, I took a flower, considered putting it in my hair, and decided to hold it instead. I was in no hurry to look like a stork wearing a bonnet.

I took my hands off the pew to pass the basket on and teetered, unused to the very high heels and dizzy from lack of food. Phoebe hissed at me, "You've been starving yourself again. You're committing suicide."

"Just cleaning out the poisons."

"Do you know what happens when you don't eat enough? Your body eats itself. You chew on your own liver."

A small, dowdy woman in the pew in front of us turned, frowned, and wagged her orchid at Phoebe. Then she turned away and wiped a lavender-scented, blue-embroidered handkerchief across her dry eyes. A little lady from Westchester, I decided. A housewife or an ex-librarian, whiling away her time producing sixty-thousand-word tracts on the course of True Love.

The minister made the sign of the cross over the heads of a few frightened doves who were lurking under the altar and the congregation sat down.

"Lydia Wentward's on cocaine," Phoebe said, whispering into my ear this time. "Isn't that wonderful?"

I grunted, not sure if that was wonderful or not, and beginning to feel dizzy for reasons other than lack of food. It had begun to occur to me, in the middle of all that unrelieved nonsense, that Myrra Agenworth was dead. I would miss her. In many ways, she had been a silly woman, vain, pampered, sentimental. She had made a great deal of money and spent it on things I would not have wanted. At times, she had even been sharp-tongued, and petty, and cynical. She had also been considerate and gentle and kind. In the five years I had known her, I had asked for her help many times. She had always given it.

I dug my hands into the pockets of my dress and clamped my teeth shut, willing myself to stay upright, willing myself to stay calm until after the service was over.

"Patience. Patience, *darling.* I've been looking all over for you."

High, whining voice, amphetamine shriek. I stopped halfway down the steps of the People's Nondenominational Church and looked around for the woman who owned it. I saw nothing but blank, deserted buildings sweating soot in the cold December air and a long, thin line of mourners come to view the body. Of course, no one could view the body. The mugger had done a job on Myrra's face and the mortician hadn't been able to correct it. The mourners didn't know that. They were fans, women from Iowa and Kansas and the deep South, come to say good-bye to the best-loved, bestselling, and best-known category romance writer in history.

The line went down the block and around the corner, out of sight. Two Moonies were working their way toward the steps, passing out pamphlets. The women took them and smiled and probably said thank you in their politest voices. A few days later they would sit on the edges of their imitation Louis Quinze chairs in a hospitality suite at the Cathay-Pierce, and smile and say thank you when somebody noticed them long enough to offer them a glass of sherry.

"Patience, for God's sake," Mary Allard said. "I've been looking for you everywhere."

She popped up in front of me, her bright little face made oddly dull by a thick wash of foundation, like the mirror with the film on it in one of those soap commercials. I didn't like Mary Allard. She was the editor-in-chief for the Passion Romance line at Acme Books, and she was always moving—diet pills and pep pills, strong Turkish coffee and Celestial Seasonings Morning Thunder Tea, vodka and marijuana and God knew what else. Myrra once wrote a novel for Passion and then had her agent, Julie Simms, audit her royalty statements. Acme had a reputation for underpaying advances, cheating on royalties, and buying up the copyrights on books whose authors were too green to know any better. Myrra had gone after Acme like a religion-crazed knight in pursuit of a dragon. She had hired private detectives, threatened to bug Acme's offices, challenged Mary Allard to a fight in the Plaza bar, and had all of Acme's records for 1975 through 1978 subpoenaed in a civil suit. Acme gave in, but Myrra didn't. She wanted proof, and she sat with her armor on until she got it. Then she took the five thousand dollars the company owed her (but had tried to say they didn't) and never spoke to Mary Allard again.

"You and Phoebe," Mary Allard said now, "I know you're both going to say you're busy, but if you'd just have dinner with me—"

"I already have plans for dinner," I said, looking around a little frantically. Phoebe was nowhere in sight, but she would be. She had come to the service in full Phoebe Damereaux regalia (black velvet caftan this time) and she was on the lookout for reporters. Reporters meant publicity, and, unlike me, she was out for all the publicity she could get. I was hoping to hide. Category romance paid my rent. My ego was supported by articles in slick women's magazines like *Sophistication* and alternative newspapers like *Left of Center*. I wrote articles on the growing incidence of alcoholism among working women, the cover-up campaign on the dangers of chemical wastes, the co-optation of women in the executive suite, and the dangers inherent in the growth of the New Right. I would continue to write them as long as no one ever found out I was also writing category romance.

I saw Janine Williams drifting away from a conversation with a middle-aged woman who had come armed with a manuscript and eyes that glowed like penlights. I waved.

Mary held on to my sleeve. "They say Phoebe wrote a book for Fires of Love," she said sweetly.

"Right," I said. Fires of Love was the new "sensual" line at Farret. Six books a month had begun appearing on the stands last Christmas. Eight books a month were planned beginning in January. Every one of them promised "more love, more romance, more sensual detail," a code for more sex.

"If Phoebe's going to write category—" Mary said.

She never got a chance to finish. Janine pulled up beside us, turned on her sweetest smile, and linked her arm through mine. The gesture should have been friendly, but it wasn't. Janine felt for Mary Allard what doctors feel for people who practice medicine unlicensed. Mary was not a real editor and should not be allowed to call herself one. Mary was not a real editor and should not be invited to all-industry conferences. Mary was not a real editor and should not be acknowledged on the street by employees of legitimate houses. Now Janine had attached herself to my arm, convinced she had the right to use me as an excuse for another round of bitchery.

"Phoebe's looking for you," Janine said, staring straight at Mary Allard. "I left her with Julie Simms. And you know what that means."

"Oh, dear," I said.

I started to disengage myself from Janine, hoping to withdraw as far as possible from her fight with Mary and the inexorable march of CBS News. If I hurried, I could get Phoebe into a cab and on the way to Luchow's before anyone even knew I was there. But Janine held on tightly, as tightly as she held on to her smile.

"Our most successful line ever," she told Mary Allard. "We think we'll gross a hundred million in the first year."

"That's good," Mary Allard said. "It's about time Farret had a line that made money."

"Exhausted," Julie Simms said, plunging into the group and pulling Phoebe behind her. Phoebe looked pink and happy, as if she'd just managed to top the *Times* bestseller list and get paid for it in chocolate. Her small, round body bounced and rippled under the black velvet, and her eyes, always dark, looked almost black.

"Isn't it terrible," Julie Simms said. "Not one relative. Not even the granddaughter."

"Ah, yes," Janine said. "She inherited all that money. Twenty million dollars, somebody said."

"'Twenty million dollars," Julie agreed. "Did you know her name was Leslie Ashe? The daughter's daughter's, I think."

"Sounds like a romance novelist," I said.

"Oh, no, no, no." Julie wrinkled her nose, making herself look even more like Doris Day than she usually did. She took her handkerchief out of her pocket and patted the grime off her forehead. "I've got to escape from Lydia," she said. "She's on something, of course, and she thinks she needs me, and I'm due for dinner with Hazel Ganz and *she* thinks her book isn't making enough money. They never think their books are making enough money."

"Books never make enough money," Phoebe said. "That's the truth."

Julie patted her arm. "Now, now. We'll get you up there one of these days. Movie contracts. Apartments in the Dakota. Vacations in Tahiti. You'll see."

She backed away and disappeared, swallowed by a tangle of newspaper photographers looking for a star. They caught Barbara Cartland and ignored us.

I didn't want to give them time to get bored or Mary Allard and Janine time to think of something else to say. I grabbed Phoebe's arm and began pulling her down the steps. There was a cab cruising east from the river, and I didn't want to lose it.

CHAPTER 2

I got home late, well after midnight, and a little drunk. I stopped at my mailbox and pulled out four letters, two from Janine, one from *Sophistication*, and one from the law firm of Hoddard, Marks, Hewitt and Long, offices at Fifty-five Broadway. I nearly stopped right there and read that one, but the vestibule where the mailboxes were was cold, and the door to the street didn't lock, and there had been a mugging already that winter. I let myself in the inner door and started making my way up the three narrow flights of steps.

Both the letters from Janine contained checks, each for twenty-five hundred dollars and each representing the second half of the advances on two Fires of Love books I'd handed in nearly four months ago. They had each taken me about a week to write, straight on the typewriter, no corrections for anything but spelling. The letter from *Sophistication* also contained a check, payment in full for an article on careers for women in the aerospace industry, which had taken me about six months to research and write. That check was for a thousand dollars.

I stopped at the first landing and turned the letter from the lawyers over and over in my hands. I was feeling cold and achy and nauseated, as if I was getting the flu to accompany my incipient hangover. The letter from the lawyers was in a very white, very stiff envelope, and it frightened me. I might have said something in an article that someone could sue me for. An editor at *Sophistication* might have changed something in an article and *made* me liable for a lawsuit. The way contracts for magazine articles ran, I'd have to pay for the lawsuit no matter who was at fault, and no matter who won in court. I leaned against the metal stair rail and ran my fingers over the raised lettering in the upper left-hand corner of the envelope. Then I put it, with the rest of the mail, into the pocket of my coat.

On the second landing, I stopped to knock on the door of 2B, the apartment directly beneath my own. The sound of a punk band wavered, momentarily wailed, then subsided. I called out a thank-you he probably couldn't hear and continued up the stairs.

On the third landing, I put my purse, used only twice since it was given to me at Christmas 1969, on the floor. I patted my pockets until I found my keys. I made resolutions, pre-New Year's, but just as futile. I would go inside, lie down on the couch, and get immediately to sleep. I would wake up in the morning and sit down to correct galley proofs of *Love's Dangerous Journey*, my Fires of Love novel for June. I would neither drink nor fast for a week.

I put my key in the lock, turned it twice, and pushed. The door opened a half inch and stopped.

It had been bolted shut from the inside.

"I don't need a locksmith," I told Carlos. "It's not the lock, it's the bolt."

He was coming reluctantly up the stairs behind me, complaining that it wasn't his problem. It probably wasn't. Carlos served four buildings on West Eighty-second Street, for which he received his apartment and what amounted to spending money. He exterminated cockroaches (as far as possible), replaced hall lights, and painted over graffiti. He periodically waited for the telephone repairman when tenants were at work or had to be out. I doubt if there was anything in my lease saying he had to break down doors when people locked themselves inside.

He stopped in front of the door and said, "How come it's bolted when you're out here?"

"It's Barbara," I told him, pointing vaguely in the direction of 3C. "She has a key. She comes in and watches HBO when I'm out."

He turned the knob and rattled the heavy metal door on its runner. The door was painted a pale pink and streaked with white. The floor was made of faded pink linoleum. Beyond that door was a nine-by-twelve room that cost me five hundred dollars a month and periodically exploded in cockroaches.

"I don't get it," he said. "The door's bolted, she's got to be in there."

"I suppose."

"Why'd she bolt the door if she was watching TV?"

I shrugged. "Barbara," I said. "You know Barbara."

Barbara was the only tenant in the building with three locks on the door, and she locked every one of them when she crossed the hall to ask for a cup of sugar. Ringing her doorbell was an adventure. She'd ask who it was, get your answer, then begin the slow process of unpeeling, the metal gears grinding and clanging in front of your nose.

"If she's in there, why doesn't she open it herself?" Carlos asked me.

"Maybe she's sick," I said. I went to sit on the stairs, drawing my legs under my dress to hide the run in my stockings. The liquor I'd drunk after dinner was beginning to turn nasty on me. The worry was making it worse. I'd stood in front of that door a good long time before going across the street to get Carlos, and I knew something had to be very wrong. Through the crack I had seen that the lights were off and the television was silent.

I pulled a pack of cigarettes from the pocket of my coat and lit one, dropping the match through the railing down the stairwell. Barbara locking herself in my apartment, even pulling the bureau out of its hiding place in my closet to cover the door, was not surprising. Barbara locking herself in my apartment and turning off all the lights was impossible. I rubbed the palms of my hands against the rough material of my dress and thought of all the things that could have gone wrong: Barbara sick with food poisoning, Barbara robbed and raped by someone coming up three flights of brick facing to the window, Barbara attacked on the street and crawling into my apartment to die. I put my cigarette, half smoked, under the heel of my shoe.

"She could be sick," I said. "Break down the door."

"It's a metal door," Carlos said. "I can't just break it down. I'll take the wood off the facing."

"It's a little door bolt," I said. "It won't matter."

He kicked timidly against the jam. "They won't pay for it," he said. "You come and ask me to kick in your door, they won't pay for it."

"So they won't pay for it. When I move, they can pay for it then."

"They'll take it out of your security deposit."

"They'll keep the security deposit anyway. Open the door."

He started hunting through his pockets for cigarettes, which he no longer kept rolled up in the sleeve of his shirt. I was thinking that someone must have told him that that went out of style in 1954, and then I stopped, tightening, staring across the hallway at 3C.

The gears ground and clanked. Metal edge scraped against metal edge.

Barbara's door was coming open, lock by lock.

The phone was ringing when the police finally got there. Barbara was sitting beside me on the stairwell, fully dressed in jeans and a turtleneck sweater. She'd been wearing a pale green robe when she first came out to find us standing in the hall, but she'd changed while she was calling the 20th Precinct. She had combed her hair and put on a fine gold chain. She had dabbed her wrists with a faint perfume.

"You ought to call Daniel," she told me. "If I were you, I'd call Daniel."

I lit three more cigarettes instead. I sat on the stairwell, watching Carlos sweat. We were all thinking the same thing: the door was bolted, someone was inside, someone was inside whom we didn't *know*. Carlos had taken a seat on the stairway just above us. If whoever was inside had a gun, he didn't want to be anywhere near it.

I stared at the cracks in the linoleum and the cracks in the plaster walls and the dim fluorescent hall light that separated Barbara's apartment from my own. I thought about how much I hated my apartment and how tired I was of fasting and how sick I felt whenever I tried to stand up. I thought about everything but what was going on behind that door.

I could live if someone stole the television set. I could buy a new typewriter. I probably should. What I didn't know was whether or not I could live in the apartment now that someone had gotten into it.

The buzzer went off and the phone began ringing at the same time. Barbara went across the hall to her apartment, unlocked all the locks, and buzzed the police through on the ground floor.

"Anybody hurt?" It was one of the officers, calling up the stairwell. I could hear doors opening above and below us, carefully secured by chains. It had been the same when Maria was mugged in the vestibule. She cried out, and no one came. When the police arrived, all the doors opened on their chains, all the tenants came to the cracks to listen.

"Rosetti," the officer said. He appeared, puffing with exertion, out of the stairwell. "This is Officer Marsh."

Officer Marsh was a pale boy who looked too young to ride a two-wheeler. He smiled shyly and scuffled his feet against the stained plaster wall. I listened to the phone while Carlos and Barbara went through their stories, interrupting each other, confusing the issue, raising their voices louder and louder. Carlos wanted to concentrate on the condition I was in when I woke him. Barbara wanted to talk about the legal aspects of forced entry. Finally, I said, "I wish whoever's in there would answer the phone."

They all turned to stare at me, and I blushed.

"It's driving me crazy," I told them. "It keeps ringing and ringing."

"Ringing and ringing," Officer Rosetti said. He did not seem much interested in me, or in my door. He was a short, dark man with thick kinky hair and deep worry lines in his forehead. I had seen him around the neighborhood, which meant he must have been assigned to the 20th Precinct for some time. "Who are you?" he asked me. "What's your name?"

"Pay McKenna," I said. The phone stopped ringing, and we both looked quickly, a little embarrassed, at the door. We turned away in unison, being careful not to look at each other. "Patience Campbell McKenna." I gave my full name. "I live in that apartment."

"Could you tell me what the problem is, please?"

The *please* was not very cordial, but I let it go. I told him about coming home after dinner with Phoebe, about the door being bolted, about Barbara coming into the hall. It wasn't much of a story. It had none of the drama and violence of a simple street robbery. There was just that door, bolted shut, and the way it had spooked us all.

"Anyone got a set of keys?" Rosetti asked.

"No one," I said. Myrra had had a set, a pair of red tin keys she kept with her own sterling silver ones on a ruby-knobbed keychain, but I didn't think that counted. Rosetti didn't care that I had given Myrra my keys the third time we met, or that when she took them she didn't know what she was doing. I had found her wandering up and down Columbus Avenue in a light rain, hatless, coatless, and minus an umbrella. She was wearing a thin, green silk dress that tied into a bow at the throat and carrying a wad of airmail paper in the palm of her hand. The airmail paper was a letter from a friend in London, saying that Myrra's daughter had died. Maybe I thought she wanted a substitute, a waif to mother in place of the now forever absent Joan. Maybe I was in need of mothering myself—my family is such a strange collection of WASP vagaries and New England eccentricities, I could be in need of anything. For whatever reason, I took Myrra by the arm and began to play the forlorn child. Myrra took my hand and my keys and guided us both to her apartment, promising to make me herb tea with honey. She was supposed to use the keys to rescue me when I was locked out. It seemed the sort of thing a mother would do, and the only promise of a future commitment I could make on such short notice. She looked old and small and lost and half dead. I wanted to leave her with *something*.

I looked up to find Officer Rosetti giving me a cross-eyed, cheek-puckered stare. He was not, I reminded myself, interested in Myrra. He had never heard of Myrra.

"Anyone got a set of keys?" he asked again.

"No one," I repeated, trying to sound louder, more confident than I had before. I managed only to sound harsh and make myself feel foolish. Then Barbara said,

"I have a set."

Everyone swung to stare at her. She held her set of keys between thumb and forefinger. They swung in the air like a hypnotist's watch.

Officer Rosetti recovered first. "You're out here," he said to Barbara.

"Of course," Barbara said.

"Were you in there? Tonight?"

"Not tonight."

"You sure? You didn't go in there accidentally, come out, lock yourself out . . ." He gave it up. The door was bolted from the inside. Somebody had to *be* inside. He turned to me. "You have a boyfriend?"

"In a way."

"He doesn't have a set of keys?"

"No."

"Could he have got hold of a set of keys? Copied yours without letting you know about it?"

"What for?"

Rosetti shrugged, looking at the door. It was beginning to spook him too.

"How the hell should I know what for?" he asked the ceiling. "How should I know why people do crazy things? They just do crazy things."

"He could have if he wanted to," I said, thinking that Daniel would not have wanted to. "But I'd have given them to him if he'd asked. That's all I can tell you."

Rosetti nodded. It was not what he wanted to hear.

"I have your permission to kick this thing in?"

"Of course," I said. "That's what I got you over here for."

Carlos looked like he was about to object, but I kicked him lightly in the ankle and he stopped before he got started. He went into the corner and folded his arms across his chest.

Rosetti stood back, drew up his right leg, and kicked. There was a crack of splintering wood and a metallic rap, and the door went flying inward.

"Damn," Rosetti said. "What did you do, paint over the windows with black? You can't see your nose in front of your face."

He leaned forward and fumbled against the wall, looking for a light switch. The neon in the ceiling coil above the sink flickered and died, flickered and died again, going into its strobe routine. Rosetti took a step forward and stopped.

"Jesus Christ," he said, "somebody killed Doris Day in a junior studio."

CHAPTER 3

It was the cat that finally took the skin off me, the very small cat that belonged to the punk rock fanatic in 2B. The punk rock fanatic must have opened his door to find out what was going on or even come out onto the stairs to watch the police. The cat walked right between Officer Marsh's legs and into the apartment.

She got halfway across my amber and gold carpet before she stopped, raised her fur, and started hissing. We all turned and stared, ignoring the blood seeping into the cracks in the fine old parquet floor, ignoring the shards of glass, the ruins of an ugly white lamp belonging to my landlord, which spread out in a semicircle under my worktable.

Detective Martinez, one of the plainclothesmen from Homicide, leaned down and picked the cat up by the scruff of its neck. He was gentle enough. I didn't have random cruelty to hold against him, although he looked capable of it. He was a short, square man with lines under his eyes and across the tops of his hands. If I'd been thinking straight, I'd have realized he was younger than I was, maybe too young for this particular murder. I was not thinking straight. The lines on his face filtered through my pain and fear and nausea and emerged monstrous.

He held out the cat to me. "This yours?"

I shook my head. I was nearing breakdown, and there were tears—the kind of tears you get right before your period or when you've had just one Scotch too many—sitting like stingers in the corners of my eyes. I wanted to leave my apartment to sit on the stairs, but I couldn't move. I wanted to escape the smell that grew stronger by the minute, but I was held by it. I tried to concentrate on the pictures of my brother and sister-in-law, my niece, and two nephews that covered one small section of an otherwise barren wall. They stood against an almost too green lawn, smiling into the late afternoon of a suburban Connecticut July.

Detective Martinez went off to give the cat to Officer Marsh and returned holding Julie Simms's appointment book, a battered, red-leather album with gold lettering on the spine.

"Now," he said, holding it open to a place near the end, "maybe we could use your friend's apartment across the hall? There were a few things I wanted to ask you—"

Martinez was unfailingly polite, unfailingly deferential, unfailingly frightening. He was half a foot shorter than I was but felt half a foot taller. His bulk seemed to block the exits. He thought I'd stabbed Julie Simms nine times in the face and neck and chest, at some point severing her carotid artery. That's what the men from the medical examiner's office were saying, that someone had severed her carotid artery. I shivered and moved away from Martinez, not sure what I was supposed to think or feel.

"We can't use Barbara's apartment," I told him. "It's a studio just like this one. She won't have anywhere to go."

"This will only take a few minutes," he tugged at me. "I don't think she'd mind for a few minutes."

I nodded and trailed him out the door and across the hall. He must have talked to Barbara at some point, but I didn't know when. I went in the door of 3C and through the tiny Pullman kitchen and sat on Barbara's immaculate white couch. I remember wondering for the five millionth time how anybody could keep a couch so white.

He sat opposite me in a green plastic upholstered chair, one I recognized as part of the landlord's early repertoire.

"Start from the beginning," he said. "Tell me what happened."

"I had dinner with a friend and came home late," I began, and went through it all again, for the third time that night. Repeating that story had become a ritual more engrossing than any High Mass. It banished everything: Julie's body, fallen in a puddle of blood and urine and feces; Martinez's suspicions; the frantic buzzing in my head.

I gave Martinez Phoebe's name and address and phone number. I told him about the funeral and listed everybody I remembered talking to there. When I came to the part about finding the door bolted, he stopped me.

"Can you think of any way that could be done?" he asked me. "How did someone get the door bolted?"

"I don't know," I said. "I thought someone was inside. Julie must have—"

He shook his head. "Not possible," he said. "In the first place, Miss Simms died in your apartment. Even if the medical examiner comes in tomorrow and says she really died by poison, she couldn't have walked three feet with the wounds she has in her. She has to have sustained those knife wounds in your apartment. Which brings us to the question of what happened to the knife."

I thought of all my shiny new kitchen knives, stuck in the butcher block holder I'd bought at Macy's.

"Somebody must have come in the window," I told Martinez, knowing I must sound like an idiot.

He just shook his head again, looking at me with eyes as big and moist as a dog whose master has died.

"The windows were both locked. Nobody came in the windows or left that way."

I began to wish I had something to hold in my hands, preferably a drink, preferably a strong one. I lit a cigarette instead, holding out the pack to offer one to Martinez.

"This is ridiculous," I told him as he pulled a pack of unfiltered Camels from his jacket pocket and lit one. "The whole thing sounds like an Agatha Christie mystery. People don't get killed in locked rooms."

"Julia Simms did."

"Julie," I corrected. "Her name was Julie Simms and she was a literary agent for romance writers and I didn't even know her that well. I've told you all this."

"And you don't know how she wound up in your apartment, stabbed at least nine times." It was a statement, not a question.

"No," I said. "I don't."

"And you don't know how the door got bolted." Another statement. He didn't sound as if he believed this one any more than he had the last.

"No," I said again. "I don't know how the door got bolted. I don't know how someone got into my apartment and locked and bolted the door and then got out again with everything shut up tight. I wish I did."

He said nothing, just staring at me for a minute, but I knew all about that trick and I wasn't going to bite. I'd used it often enough myself, when I was interviewing someone who did not want to be interviewed or getting information I had no business having. Most people can't stand silence. Stare at them without saying a word, and they'll talk and talk. Sometimes they'll even tell you all the things they had no intention of telling you.

After a while, Martinez flipped open Julie's appointment book and stared at a page.

"You say you saw Miss Simms this afternoon? At a funeral?"

"That's right," I said. "At Myrra Agenworth's funeral. Myrra Agenworth was a category romance novelist. Julie—"

"What's a category romance novelist?"

"Someone who writes category romances," I said. "A category romance is like a Harlequin, you know. They're short, they're written to a formula. Actually, Myrra wrote family sagas, too, but—"

"That's all right," Martinez said. "When was this funeral? From what time to what time?"

"From four-thirty to about six," I said. "It was a very long service. But I didn't actually see her at the service, I saw her afterwards, on the church steps. She was with Phoebe Weiss, the woman I had dinner with."

Martinez consulted the notebook. "I have a Phoebe Damereaux. No Weiss."

"Same person." His eyebrows shot up, and I blushed. "People don't usually write romance novels under their own names," I explained. "Phoebe Damereaux is Phoebe Weiss's pseudonym."

"All right," he nodded. "Do you know any of the rest of these people? Hazel Ganz?"

"Julie was supposed to have dinner with someone named Hazel Ganz. A client, I think. I only know her by sight."

"Amelia S."

"Amelia Samson," I said. "She's—"

"I know who Amelia Samson is. The one with the castle."

"That's right. I think her real name is Joan Wroth, but I'm not absolutely sure."

"What about someone named Mary A? There's a rude little drawing—"

"Well, yes," I said. "I expect there would be. That's Mary Allard, she's editor of the Passion Romance line at Acme. But Julie wouldn't be doing business with her, not now."

"Why not now?"

"Because this Allard woman cheated a few of Julie's clients, and Julie found out about it, and there were audits and lawsuits. It was silly, really, because any one category romance book doesn't make that much money. It's the line as a whole that makes money, so you want to keep your writers happy so they'll go on writing books for the series. And what happened with Mary is that she or someone in her company falsified royalty statements, and when Julie found out about it, Passion lost most of their best writers."

"But this Allard woman didn't lose her job?"

"Oh, no," I said. "Acme has a reputation—well, let's just say the company probably applauded her for it, if you get what I mean."

He stared off into space, lost in private speculations. Nasty-minded speculations, too, I thought, and vowed to be quieter and less eager to please. I didn't count on his dropping a bomb in my lap.

"How about this one?" he asked. "Leslie Ashe."

"Leslie *Ashe?*" I could hear my voice squeak and practically feel the eyes bulge out of my head. "But that's not *possible.*"

"Why not?"

"Leslie Ashe is Myrra's granddaughter. She isn't even in the country. She didn't come for the funeral. She lives in England."

Martinez looked down at Julie's appointment book.

"Leslie Ashe," he recited. "Breakfast at the Plaza Hotel, seven A.M., Friday, eleven December. That's about three hours from now."

What Daniel said was, "Did you give them this number? If you're coming right here, you must have given this number."

I sat curled up in the ugly green plastic chair, drinking very strong tea with lemon and sugar from one of Barbara's white china cups. It was not very good china, but china is not one of the things Barbara spends money on. She does spend money on teas, and the kind she gave me was rich and dark and electric. I was coming awake, even if it was five o'clock in the morning.

"You can come here if you want," Daniel was saying. "I won't leave you to sleep in the street." He let out a strained, artificial little whinny. "I have to leave for work at seven-thirty, but you could at least have a shower."

"Right," I said, beginning to wish I'd called Phoebe. But I didn't need Phoebe just then, I needed Daniel. Or I needed what Daniel was supposed to be, which he was not. After three years, I should have known that much and usually did. Tonight there was a dead woman in my apartment and a policeman waiting in the hall, and I wanted comfort. I didn't want to remind him how often I had *provided* comfort.

"Well," he coughed. "You could come and crash here tomorrow and not go out of the apartment. I guess that would be all right. Unless," his voice brightened, "unless you have appointments. Do you have appointments?"

"I don't know," I said. "I'm supposed to come in and sign my statement to the police. I don't know if that's tomorrow."

"I won't be home till after nine," Daniel said doubtfully. "This is the last big push, you know. I should hear about the partnership right after New Year's."

"You've told me," I said. Daniel is a very senior associate at the law firm of Cravath, Swaine, and Moore. He either made partner this year or he was out. I sent up a small prayer that somehow, somewhere, all the money that had gone to Saint Paul's and Amherst and the Harvard

Law School would result in nothing more impressive than a two-room office three floors above the main street in Akron, Ohio.

"Maybe you should go to Phoebe's," Daniel said brightly. "She always sleeps late."

"Maybe I should," I said. I dropped the receiver back into the cradle without bothering to say good-bye. It was not like Daniel to be so blatantly insensitive. His selfishness was usually cloaked in philosophy. We did not have keys to each other's apartments because he did not believe in "the blurring of independent lives." He also did not believe in the enforced remembrance of birthdays and anniversaries and what he called "the commercialization of Christmas," a sentiment that seemed to apply solely to trips to see the tree lit up in Rockefeller Center. I had been with him three years and still had no idea why. He was a very beautiful man, fine-boned and strong of body. I was used to him.

I fumbled through my coat for cigarettes and came up instead with the mail. I dropped the envelopes into my lap and didn't bother to go chasing after the check that went fluttering to the floor. I concentrated instead on the letter from Hoddard, Marks, Hewitt and Long. It reminded me of Daniel.

I picked at the corner until it tore. Bad news is supposed to come in threes, I thought. Might as well get it over with. I pulled out the single sheet of heavy letterhead and unfolded it on my lap.

"Dear Miss McKenna," it read, "I am writing to request your attendance, as one of the beneficiaries, at the reading of the will of Susan Marie DeFord, a.k.a. Myrra Agenworth, on Monday, December 14 at 2:30 P.M. in the offices of . . ."

CHAPTER 4

Julie Simms had a baby. It was eighteen months old, a girl, and lived with Julie's mother in an apartment in Gramercy Park. There was also a husband, very young and still very much alive, either in a detox center someplace or sleeping in a doorway in the Bowery. The husband had money but no family. The Chase Manhattan Bank paid the income from his trust fund directly into a checking account, and the checking account was depleted by the ravages of drink. Or the evils of rum, if you will. That was the Gospel According to Lydia Wentward. I got back at her by calling her "Ellie" (her real name was Elspeth Hoag) and hung up to consider what I was going to do with the rest of the afternoon.

I was in Phoebe's apartment, theoretically in seclusion. Phoebe was out on a round of visits to publishers, agents, and Italian restaurants. I picked at the cheese blintzes she had left warming for me in the oven and answered the phone.

The Gospel According to Amelia Samson: Julie's husband was indeed alive and indeed an alcoholic, which was to be expected, since Julie was more successful than he was. He wanted to get a divorce and start a normal life, but she refused because she was Catholic and because she secretly loved him. Some tragedy in her childhood (a father unfaithful to the mother, Amelia thought) made it impossible for her to trust men. Julie therefore needed her career and her husband, which was exactly what the husband could not accept. He got her into my apartment and stabbed her to death so he could give up drinking and make a fresh start with a woman who respected the vocation of wife and mother.

The Gospel According to Mary Allard: Julie Simms was not now and

never had been married. She had her baby out of wedlock because she
was thirty-four when she got pregnant and was afraid she'd never get
the chance again. This had nothing to do with her murder. Julie Simms
was murdered either by Janine Williams or Lydia Wentward, both of
whom were in Big Trouble, although Mary didn't know about what.
She knew about the trouble because Julie had hinted as much to her,
when she made a lunch appointment last week.

The Gospel According to Melissa "Muffy" Arnold Whitney, Rye
Country Day School, Farmington Class of '69, Vassar Class of '73,
Junior Assemblies, Westchester Cotillion, Cosmopolitan Club and now
managing editor of *Sophistication,* which is exactly the job her mother
had in 1951, when she found out she was pregnant with Muffy and (of
course) had to give it all up: I just heard about it and it's *terrible,* I feel
so sorry for you, you must be so *uncomfortable* being in all the papers
like this, but of course it's a *perfect* story for us now that we're so
involved in these lady executive murders, it's going on all over the
country, these men just hate women who carry briefcases, I never
touch one anymore, but of course Sheree Hyland's working on it and
she's not worried and she wants to interview you so could you come in
Thursday at eleven and bring the "Taking Off" copy with you? I know
it isn't supposed to be due until after New Year's but I've got this *hole*
in the March issue, these writers from California are so *unprofessional,*
and anyway I can't thank you enough and I'll see you then.

The Gospel According to Phoebe (Weiss) Damereaux (delivered by
phone from Mamma Leone's during the lunch rush): everybody in
town is figuring out where you are, and you should *not* be answering
the phone. These people are going to hound you to death. Also, you
should heat up the chicken in the blue and white Corning Ware casse-
role on the third shelf in the refrigerator, because if you insist on living
on black coffee and Merit cigarettes, you're going to be dead of starva-
tion before we get this thing straightened out. Also also, I talked to My
Friend the Lawyer, and we'll meet you for dinner at Oenophilia at
seven-thirty. Reservations in the name of Carras. Also also also, Lydia
called *(very* high on some kind of *pep* pills) and said that Julie's husband was a drunk and he came through the window of your apartment

and stabbed her with a broken bourbon bottle. This doesn't sound like what you told me.

"Not drunk," Janine Williams said, when I finally managed to tear myself away from the phone and make my appointment at Farret. "Parkinson's disease. *Parkinson's disease.*"

She put her hand up and patted her hair into place, ignoring an elaborate board game going on in the hallway. It had been set up by a number of Bright Young Men from Marketing, and as far as I could tell consisted of thin, penlight-like wands which, when applied to the surface of a Plexiglas board cover, caused small discs to hover in the air like flying saucers.

"All the gossip is so malicious," Janine said, wandering down the hall toward her office. Her path was blocked in several places by stand-up displays of romance books, including one with a three-dimensional pop-up of Amelia Samson looking blue. "Drunkenness and divorce and all this nonsense. Lydia even had the man sleeping in a doorway in the Bowery, which is perfectly ridiculous. Julie didn't put him in the hospital until last year."

"Mr. Simms is in the hospital?"

Janine nodded vaguely. "A sanatorium somewhere in Westchester," she said, staring at her nameplate on the hollow plywood door of her office. For a moment, she was fixed. It was a moment that went on much too long. All the unease I had left in Phoebe's apartment, all the nausea from the moment I had found Julie Simms on my floor, began to wash in on me. Then the mood broke, and Janine pushed open her office door and stood back to let me walk through. "A very expensive place, I heard," she said, still thinking of Julie's husband. "That was all right as long as Julie was out earning money. What happens now, I don't know."

I sat down in a very uncomfortable chair and pulled my feet up under me, looking past the mountain of computer printouts on Janine's desk to a corkboard covered with colored three-by-five cards that hung on the wall beside the single file cabinet. One of those cards was for *Love's Dangerous Journey,* corrected galleys for which were due more than a week ago and now resided in a marked manila envelope at the

20th Precinct. There had been blood on them, and the police wanted to know whose.

"I can't understand why everyone's having so much trouble with these reports," Janine said, patting the stack of printouts. "People look at them and say 'computer' and then shut right down. These should make it *easier* to understand what's going on."

"I never read reports," I said. "I can't understand why anyone would want to."

"Oh, not you," Janine said. "Writers never read anything if it doesn't have their names on it. I mean my editors. I have three editors. I have reports that tell them what's selling and what isn't selling. Where it's selling and where it isn't selling. And they act like it doesn't matter. For a *romance* line."

I leaned over and looked at the first page of the printout, upside down.

"These tell you what books sold where, when, and how? You can tell by just looking at them?"

"*I* can tell. The front *office* can tell. My associate editors are waiting to be presented with hardbound ledgers signed in quill pens."

"So am I," I said. "Don't send me one."

"I won't. Not unless you ask for one. Or your agent asks for one."

"I don't have an agent. I have a problem."

I took my cigarettes out, lit one, then groped around in the mess on Janine's desk for the Vassar College ashtray. I wanted to ask her if she knew Muffy Arnold Whitney, but I stopped myself. Janine had been at Vassar what Phoebe had been at Greyson: the poor girl at the rich girl's school, the uncomfortable reminder of difference in the midst of privilege. Phoebe had accepted the role cheerfully and lived with it easily— and blown our assumptions to pieces whenever she needed something to do. Janine exuded a nervous defensiveness. She had to be ten years older than Phoebe or I—and twenty years out of college—but she pressed her credentials on us, gently but insistently, almost every time we met.

She pressed them on me now, in the form of plaques and pictures cluttering the top of her desk. The pictures were all in silver frames and most of them were signed. I stared vaguely at one of Janine in an evening dress that looked like a shirtwaist, surrounded by Phoebe, Amelia, Lydia, Myrra, and Julie in varying degrees of exuberantly ostentatious dress. I was about to ask what it was a picture *of* when I finally focused on her face. She was looking at me with the exaggerated concern of someone who wants to be empathetic, but who finds herself faced with a problem so alien as to be unimaginable. If I had come to Janine with a chapter that wouldn't work, a contract foul-up, a copyright problem, she would have been all energy and sincerity. Janine's commitment to Being An Editor rivaled Thomas Becket's to the Roman Catholic Church. The murder of an agent in an Upper West Side studio made her go blank.

I was feeling a little blank myself. The combination of lack of sleep and nagging guilt—although I had no idea what I was feeling guilty of —was making my eyes water and my vision blur. I explained as clearly as possible about the galleys and why I didn't have them, then sat back and let my eyes wander around the room.

Like most large publishing companies, Farret relegated its romance division to the darkest and least accessible quarters in the building. Not only did Janine and her staff have to share space with Marketing and Sales, but they were assigned the cramped, windowless cubicles in the core block of the floor. In place of a view of Gramercy Park, Janine had a framed sales chart showing the relative profitability of the four Farret romance lines under her control. The red vein symbolizing Fires of Love was shorter, but significantly higher, than all the others.

"Looks nice, doesn't it?" Janine said. "If it hadn't been for Fires of Love, Farret would probably be out of the romance business altogether."

"The blue one doesn't seem to be doing too well," I said, having to squint to see anything at all. "Seems to have been cut off in its prime."

"Romantic Life," Janine said, wrinkling her nose in disgust. "We folded it around the time we started Fires of Love. That was really a disaster, that line. Innocent virgins swooning at a single glance and probably passing out cold on their wedding nights, for all anyone could tell. Two months after that line hit the supermarkets, one of the soaps had its goody-goody character give birth to miscegnated triplets while her husband went to Switzerland for a sex change operation."

"I didn't think there was such a thing as a romance line that didn't make money," I said.

"They all make money," Janine said. "Some of them just don't make enough money. You know how these people are. If you don't have a 40 percent profit margin, you're sullying their pristine literary reputations for no good reason."

"Maybe what I ought to do is write for the soaps." I leaned back and closed my eyes. "Do screenplays for soft-core porn—"

"Now, now." Janine started straightening papers on her desk. "What you ought to do is stop at the desk and pick up your extra set of galleys, then go do whatever it was you were going to do anyway. Go on living a normal life."

"All right," I said. "What I was going to do today, before somebody decided to kill Julie Simms on my floor, was go to the animal shelter and get a cat."

"What?"

"A cat." I opened my eyes, wishing I didn't have to. "I've been wanting a cat. I was going to go and get one."

Janine looked nonplussed, but she could not stop being Janine. She gave me the brightest smile she could manage, forced an encouraging note into her voice and said, "Well, good. A cat. Maybe you could bring it to the cocktail party on Sunday."

CHAPTER 5

The galleys were not waiting at the desk when I got there. The rabbity little editorial assistant who manned the station wasn't inclined to look for them, so I picked up a copy of Phoebe's *Wild, Haunting Melody* and started wandering down the hall toward Marketing. According to the best inside intelligence, the first of the "good parts" started on page thirty. It was not as good a "good part" as the one that started on page 106. *That* one, according to a pious-looking little girl I met in the Fifth Avenue B. Dalton's, was "not describable in words." I bet. I'd never had the courage to ask Phoebe if she made these things up or actually practiced them.

"What would you do," Martin Caine asked me, "if I threw myself off this chair into your arms?"

"Catch you, put you down, and pat your head," I said.

"Figures."

He made a stab at attaching a streamer of red crepe paper to the top of the doorjamb and missed. Even standing on a chair, Marty Caine was *short*. He was in perfect proportion, he was very attractive, and he had the air of a prematurely cynical Frank Sinatra, but he was five five. If that. The first time I saw him, he was sitting down. I nearly made a move. Then he stood up, and I had to restrain myself from ruffling his curly brown hair and offering him a teddy bear.

I reached up and held the crepe paper in place. He slammed a copy of *Cashelmara* over the tack and jumped to the floor.

"Jesus," he said. "Last year I was ready to hang up mourning, for God's sake. Can you believe that?"

"You didn't think Fires of Love was going to work?" I went into his office and sat on his desk. He was in Marketing, so he got a window.

He was the Marketing Director for category romance, so he got exactly *one* window.

"Hell," he said, coming in after me, "who knows what's going to work? If you want to know the truth, no. I didn't think Fires of Love was going to work. The Advisory Board business was okay—getting writers to help with the tip sheet, promote the line, I liked that. But Janine didn't take any of their suggestions, and she's had a couple of failures. I kept thinking there were twenty or thirty lines out there, about half of them just like Fires of Love. Why buy us? But I really wasn't thinking much. I was too busy being buried under the last debacle."

"Good old Romantic Life."

"Good old Romantic Life." He leaned back in his swivel chair and put his feet on the desk. He gestured to my copy of *Wild, Haunting Melody.* "You get to page 106 yet?"

"I just picked it up in the hall."

"That's what I want to do in my next life. Be Phoebe's publicity person. No more late nights, no more working weekends, no more 'why isn't this book selling as well as we thought it would.' Phoebe's books always sell, you'd have a hard time keeping her out of the magazines, and she's always *nice.* From what I hear, she even cooks for you."

"Only when she's keeping kosher." I didn't tell him that Phoebe's keeping kosher never once kept her out of Mamma Leone's. "I think all you people get much too excited," I told him. "So a romance line makes 5 percent instead of 50. As long as it's not losing money—"

Marty nearly choked. "Oh, God," he said. "You must have been talking to Janine. She's very big on this keep-a-good-front business. Well, let me tell you. Romantic Life not only lost money, it lost a mint. It lost so much money, it was so embarrassingly bad, there are still booksellers who won't talk to us. I nearly had to hire hit men to convince some of the stores to carry Fires of Love." He jumped up from the desk. "Before Romantic Life, we had such a good reputation, I was getting romance books into stores that didn't carry romance books. It was great. Snobby little bookstores in Westchester, back-to-the-land bookstores in Vermont. It was wonderful for the genre—"

"Everyone's always talking about what's wonderful for the genre," I said. "The whole thing makes me tired. Have you ever thought it might be a pulp genre? That where it belongs is in the supermarkets? That there's nothing necessarily *wrong* with that?"

"Maybe," Marty said. "But let's face it, Pay. There's good trash and there's bad trash. Every other genre but romance has been able to figure that out. There are great mystery novels. There are great horror novels. There are great sci-fi novels. People think romance readers are stupid, and they give them what they think romance readers want, and they get Romantic Life."

"Okay, okay," I said. "I agree the level of contempt is annoying."

"The level of contempt is ridiculous. People may not be able to tell you why something is good or bad, but they know. They may take a bad book if it's the only one of its kind, but when you've got the companies putting out ninety books a month and a lot of them are upping the quality control by light-years with every volume, they're not going to be talked down to. Look at Phoebe. Phoebe writes—"

"Marty." I grabbed his wrist, trying to make him stop moving. "You don't have to sell me. I write the stuff."

"Right." He sat down and put his legs on the desk again. "Sorry. I don't understand publishing people. They take one look at a book that's selling well and act like dogs who've just had their noses pushed in their own shit."

I got out of my chair and started gathering up my things. If Phoebe wasn't determined to marry Jewish and Marty addicted to six-foot blondes, I could fix them up with each other. I spent a lot of time thinking about it.

"I'm going to get out of here," I said. "You going to be at the conference?"

"Oh, yeah." He had lapsed into something that looked like boredom. "You remember Lydia Wentward's Asian tour last fall? She's got pictures, and she wants blowups. Six feet by five feet. I'm not kidding."

"Sounds like Lydia."

"Yeah."

I was halfway back to the editorial assistant when he yelled, "Pay? I don't think you did it."

The galleys were waiting for me at the desk, wrapped in a large manila envelope. The editorial assistant had her back to me. Her neck was stiff with the rage that infects all graduates of the Seven Sisters who discover that, Phi Beta Kappa or no Phi Beta Kappa, in publishing you start by typing.

I put the package in my tote bag, took a copy of *Romantic Times*, and stopped to look at a large oil painting leaning from the top of a low set of bookshelves to the concrete wall. The painting was obviously "cover art" for a Fires of Love book. The hero and heroine were in a much too compromising position for any other romance line. What interested me was the lovingly detailed two-masted schooner in the foreground. Someone had stuck an infinitesimal outboard motor to its ass.

I took the elevator to the ground floor. Farret has one of those newsstands that carry every magazine published on four continents, every newspaper available in the United States plus *The Times* of London, and a judicious selection of paperback fiction. I bought six Agatha Christies, nine Nicholas Blakes, and every Dorothy L. Sayers, P. D. James, and Emma Lathen they had. I also bought their entire stock of New York *Posts*—the edition with "baffled" in the headlines. I put the books in my bag and hefted the *Posts* into my arms. Then I walked out into the late afternoon gray of Madison Avenue and dumped the newspapers into the nearest trash can.

I was standing on the northeast corner of East Thirty-fifth and Madison, trying to hail a cab in the lightly falling snow, when a young, brown-haired woman next to me turned to the man whose arm she was holding and said, "Maybe that's *why* Julie Simms is dead. Bobby, I'm telling you, something is wrong and I know it."

Just then a cab pulled up and I fell into it. We were halfway uptown on our way to the animal shelter before I realized I knew who the woman was.

Hazel Ganz.

CHAPTER 6

"Oh," the girl at the animal shelter said, "that one. I must admit, we haven't had a lot of hope for that one."

She put her hands into the cage and came out with a kitten just under five inches long, very uncertain on its legs, and scared witless.

"It's weaned," the girl said, "but just. And they're supposed to be housetrained, but I think it must be a little early for this one." She held it up to her nose and shook her head. "And she's listless. I don't think we'd have held on to her, but she's so *small.*"

"She's so *black,*" I said, taking the cat in my hands. It didn't like being in the air and said so, so I put it in the breast pocket of my shirt. I did this on the principle that if human babies are calmer when they can hear a heartbeat, the technique ought to work as well for cats.

"There are papers to fill out," the girl said, pulling fretfully at her string tie. "And of course the fee. When she's ready to be spayed, you just bring her right back and we'll take care of it for you. People are so irresponsible. You have no idea how many *thousands* of unwanted cats are born in this city *every year.*"

She gave me a fierce glare, as if I had been personally responsible for at least a third of that number, then turned on her heel and walked away. Although she was well under thirty, she was dressed as the proto-typical old maid. Her shoes laced up to her ankles. Her dress, made of a dingy calico busy with sentimentalized approximations of cornflowers, fell below her knees and rose high on her throat, ending in a fussy ruffle that spilled over her flat chest. Even her granny glasses looked like they'd come out of her great aunt's attic.

I let her go off and began to wander around on my own. Except for a mother nursing six kittens, the cats were all in individual cages, each

with its mound of sawdust in the corner, each with its identical tin
dinner and water bowl set. They looked miserable. Well-fed, well-cared
for, much-petted cats affect a pose of supercilious self-sufficiency. Left
alone for twenty-four hours with nothing more than food for the dura-
tion and the carpet to shred, they behave like four-year-olds sent to bed
without supper. I rubbed the heads of a few of the especially ugly ones
as I passed. No one adopts an ugly cat from the animal shelter. No one
wants some pink-eyed, white-haired, flat-faced monstrosity curling up
at their feet after dinner. God only knows what happens to them.

I turned the corner and found myself in a room of dogs, their cages
low and close to the ground, their voices sharp with eagerness, their
eyes painfully hopeful. I petted only the smaller ones. Although I grew
up with large dogs—my father could not imagine life without a Great
Dane sitting erect beside his chair, keeping him company during the
six o'clock news—I am invariably afraid of them. I restrict myself to
beagles and basset hounds and collies, the last of which can be very
vicious. I once saw a collie bite the head off a kitten who'd done no
more than try to make friends. I was only thirteen, it was a kitten I was
particularly fond of, and the incident should have put me off collies
forever, but it didn't. *Lassie* was the first and only television show I was
allowed to watch as a child. It was magic.

I had my hands on the head of a very un-Lassie-like collie when I saw
the cocker spaniel. It was sitting in the far corner of what I first
thought was an empty cage, half buried in sawdust and shaking like a
tremor in the San Francisco Bay. With the small cat in my pocket
protesting loudly, I leaned over and reached out to the dog, making
cooing noises like a demented nanny. The only effect it had was to kick
up an even more violent trembling in the corner. I had to do a full
waist bend just to get within reach of the dog's head.

Almost as soon as I touched it, it stopped shaking. It sniffed around
for a moment, worrying my fingers with its nose, then shook the sawdust clear as if it were water and began to crawl across the cage to me.
The rhinestones in its collar winked in the harsh overhead light. The
pink ribbons in its ears drooped to the floor. A red and white flash
glittered at its throat.

Myrra's dog.

With one of Myrra's earrings caught in its collar.

I rang the bell for the attendant.

"This dog," the mock-spinster said, "is a female who has had *puppies.*" She gave me the kind of accusatory glare I'd always associated with snake oil salesmen who preach about sin.

"She had a litter of six," I said. "They all went to very nice mansions in Westchester."

"I'm sure. And I'm sure the puppies had puppies who went to very good homes, too. The ones we find wandering around in garbage cans are the result of spontaneous generation."

"Of course," I said. "I can see what you're up against." I couldn't imagine Esmeralda rooting around in garbage cans. Myrra had given that dog all the affection and luxury she had been unable to give her daughter when her daughter was growing up, and Myrra, newly divorced, was first trying to write. I had never known Myrra to indulge herself as she indulged Esmeralda. Esmeralda's tastes were so refined that, although she loved caviar, she would only eat beluga, and although she loved chocolates, she would only eat Godiva raspberry creams. Esmeralda had a mink hat and jacket with her initials on the hand-carved wooden buttons; a down sleep cushion whose covers, each made of a different pastel silk, were changed daily; and a Steuben glass dinner dish.

At the moment, she had a case of the nerves and a very small cat. The cat was sleeping on Esmeralda's head, which seemed to make them both happy.

"She'll have to go in for spaying *right away,*" the spinster said.

I took the pen she held out to me and shook my head.

"I don't think I can promise that," I said. "The woman she belonged to wouldn't have approved of it."

"The woman she belonged to doesn't have any say in the matter. She *abandoned* the poor creature. We cannot have this city overrun with *domesticated* animals with no conception of how to survive in the wild—"

"Central Park West is hardly the wild," I said. "And Myrra didn't abandon the dog. She took it out for a walk and got mugged in Riverside Park. We've all been looking for Esmeralda for over a week."

"Mugged," the woman said.

"Murdered," I smiled.

"Just a minute." She disappeared through a low, narrow door and returned a moment later with a shoebox. "You have to understand this is a most unusual situation," she said. "This dog came to us a little over a week ago. As you can see, she is not wearing a license."

"Well, of course not," I said. "If she was wearing a license, wouldn't somebody have got in touch with Myrra or the family?"

"Certainly. But she was not wearing a license. She was, however, dressed up in these ridiculous garments—" The hat and jacket came whipping out of the shoebox. "She was also tied very carefully to our porch. A baby in a basket, so to speak."

"Well, maybe someone found her wandering," I said. "They just thought this was the best place to bring her."

"Unlikely. It is the lurid belief of most of the residents of the City of New York that we gas our animals here."

"But still—"

"But still. But still, I opened the office myself that morning, at six. Of course, I didn't actually open the office, but I came in to do some work. The last person to leave the night before locked up well after three. I simply do not believe that some Good Samaritan was wandering around this neighborhood between three and six on a December morning, tying dogs to doorknobs with granny knots."

"What December morning?" I asked, feeling a little faint. "When?"

She pulled out a file card and adjusted her glasses on her nose, the time-honored gesture of Mrs. Grundys and maiden lady civics teachers everywhere.

"The second," she said. "December second."

"If you'd just murdered somebody," I asked the cabdriver, "and that somebody had a dog with them, would you take the dog to the animal shelter and leave it there?"

"If I'd just *murdered* somebody?" We were stuck in traffic just above the World Trade Center, seemingly for good. Esmeralda was in a carrier on the cab floor. Camille (the cat) was in my pocket, her empty carrier beside me on the seat. I had to do something to take my mind off the time. I had promised Mr. Grandison, senior partner at Hoddard, Marks, Hewitt and Long, and executor of Myrra's estate, that I would be in his office by six.

"If you were a mugger," I said, "and you mugged someone in Riverside Park. And you murdered the person you mugged. Would you take the dog she had with her and take it to the animal shelter and tie it up there?"

"You writing one of those murder mystery novels?" the cabdriver said. "My wife likes those murder mystery novels. Different from detective stories. I used to like detective stories. Philo Vance. You know about him?"

"Sort of." The last murder mystery I'd read was an Agatha Christie I'd picked up in the Milan airport during my obligatory backpacking tour around Europe after college graduation. I was hot, dirty, exhausted, and trying to fly Alitalia standby to Rome in the middle of July. The Agatha Christie was a French translation, and the last two pages were missing. Of course, there were the books in my bag, but I hadn't read them.

"Muggers are mostly short skinny guys," the cabdriver said. "Eunuchs, you know. They get that way from all the dope. Can't hurt you."

"Muggers never kill anybody?"

"Sure they do. I just don't understand how."

"Right."

There was a break in the traffic, a very small break, but enough. He floored the gas pedal and shot through, maneuvering us onto the nearly empty southbound side of Broadway.

"Wasn't the animal shelter where I picked you up?" he asked me.

"It's right around the corner from there," I said.

"And you're talking a mugging in Riverside Park?"

"Riverside in the Eighties."

"You're saying this mugger is going to kill a guy in Riverside Park in the Eighties, then walk a dog to Second and Fifty-ninth and tie it up outside the animal shelter."

"Exactly," I said. "That's exactly what I'm saying."

We pulled up outside a heavy, dirty-brown building that looked like the cross between an Italianate mausoleum and a monument to the Glory that was Greece.

"Nah," the cabdriver said. "Like I said, muggers are these skinny little guys. Puerto Ricans. Ninety-pound weaklings. They don't know about dogs."

I tipped him a dollar. I didn't mention that I hadn't needed his advice. No mugger was going to take a mink-clad cocker spaniel with a rhinestone collar and a leather leash all the way across town to tie it to the doorknob of the animal shelter. Not at three o'clock in the morning, he wasn't.

At least, I didn't think so.

CHAPTER 7

Hoddard, Marks, Hewitt and Long had the fourteenth, fifteenth, six-teenth, and seventeenth floors of the Hogarth Building, as the mauso-leum was called, and private elevators going to each one. The elevators had brass doors and tired old men in blue-jacketed uniforms to operate them. They were entirely filled by secretaries and paralegals on their way out the door and into the subway and home to Queens and the Upper East Side respectively. Both groups looked like they spent a great deal of time reading *Mademoiselle,* but different parts of it.

A blue-jacketed functionary beckoned me, and I piled into a polished brass and red damask cage. I had decided to come to Hoddard, Marks, Hewitt and Long because I thought the earring, which was probably valuable, most properly belonged to the estate. Myrra, like most women not born to wealth, had had no use for paste, and if her taste consisted of an unwavering devotion to brand names, that didn't make the things she owned any less expensive. Jewelry came from Harry Winston, glassware from Steuben. The entire history of European painting was reduced to Degas and Bosch, but every piece of property was authentic, irreplaceable, and accompanied by a documentation folder that rivaled the FBI file on Eldridge Cleaver. It was also un-doubtedly willed to someone. The lawyer would know to whom.

Even so, going up in the elevator, I was uneasy. I had a feeling the police had known all along that Myrra's death was not an ordinary mugging. I could see the discrepancies. It *was* ridiculous for a woman Myrra's age to decide to walk her dog at two-thirty in the morning, and it wasn't in character. Myrra wrote at dawn. She had put herself to bed at eleven o'clock every night of her life for the past twenty years. Guests were invited for dinner at seven and unceremoniously ushered out at quarter past ten. Why would she get dressed to the teeth and go wandering off to Riverside Park four and a half hours after her normal bedtime?

I blinked. I had somehow got off the elevator, and now I was standing in a fifty-thousand-dollar sea of Persian rug. The girl behind the wide-bellied cherrywood desk was very young and very thin and very angry. I didn't blame her. It was Friday.

"I have an appointment with Mr. Grandison," I said. "I'm Pay McKenna."

"Of course." She made it sound as if she knew perfectly well who I was and exactly how late. Since I never wear a watch, I couldn't tell. "Mr. Grandison is on the phone," she said. "If you'll just take a seat, he'll be with you in a moment."

I looked around at the seats, mostly black leather chairs shined to look like polished ebony. I didn't think they'd benefit from Esmeralda's attention, and I said so.

"Technically," the girl said, "you shouldn't bring a dog in here at all. Unless it's a Seeing Eye dog. Is it a Seeing Eye dog?"

"Of course not."

"I didn't think so."

"It's part of the property I'm delivering to Mr. Grandison," I said. "It belonged to a client of his."

A light went on on her telephone and she turned away to answer it.

"A dog," she said. "In a box." There was a silence, during which she sniffed a little and did rabbit imitations with her nose. "Of course," she said at last. "Of course. Right away." She stood up and smiled at me, the way secretaries smile to let you know you've made an enemy for life. "If you'll come this way, please."

She led me out of the reception area and down a long corridor lined with cherrywood doors, each sporting a single brass nameplate. The names on the nameplates sounded like a WASP hall of fame—Hewitt, Alden, Ingersoll, Winthrop, Whitney, Renfrew, Standish, Hayes. In this company, McKenna sounded a little foreign, and Weiss/Damereaux was unthinkable.

She stopped in front of a door with "Grandison" on the nameplate and knocked softly. I didn't hear anything, but she must have, because she turned the knob and stuck her head in.

"Mr. Grandison?" she said. "I have Miss McKenna."

A mumble. I started to wonder just how elaborate this ritual could get. Would we still be here a week from now, invisibly bowing back and forth through a barrier of cherrywood and brass?

The girl suddenly stood aside and threw the door wide, revealing a very small, very fat man behind a desk much too large for him. He rose to greet me, his well-padded hands outstretched, his smile thick and nervous. Fat-lipped, fat-bellied, and droopy-eyed, I noticed. Myrra must have hated the man. Although she could never tell if her women friends were pretty or plain, she had unyielding requirements for men.

"Miss McKenna," Mr. Grandison said, trying hard to beam. "Do sit down. I hope you had a pleasant afternoon."

I nodded, not knowing what to say to that. He sat down behind his desk, where he looked like a power-mad, slightly maniacal dwarf.

"What is this?" he said. "You've found Miss DeFord's dog?"

It took me a minute to remember that Myrra's real name had been Susan Marie DeFord and to convince myself that I had not somehow arrived in the wrong place to talk to a man who wouldn't understand a word I was saying. I put Esmeralda's carrier on the desk and opened it. She was shivering with panic and nipped me twice before I managed to get her positioned on Mr. Grandison's blotter.

"The dog and the earring," I told him. "I was more worried about the earring than the dog." I didn't say I was perfectly capable of taking care of the dog.

I ran my hand along Esmeralda's collar and unhooked the earring. It was hard to do. The post had become tangled in the dog's hair, and the facets of some of the stones were caught in the hollows near the clasp.

I put the ruby and diamond pear in front of Mr. Grandison. He didn't even look at it.

"Of course," he said. "I can't possibly discuss the terms of the will at this time."

"That's all right," I said. "I'll wait till Monday. What I wanted to discuss was—"

"I will tell you it was a very old will," Grandison said. "Made nearly four years ago. It was very unusual for Miss DeFord to let four years go by without making a new will."

"I'm not surprised," I said. "She couldn't let a month go by without making a new funeral service. No, Mr. Grandison, it's about the earring—"

"It was a very unusual will," Grandison said dreamily. He was staring at the ceiling, oblivious not only to the earring but to the fact that Esmeralda was getting ready to permanently mark his felt desk blotter. "Not that she cut her own family, of course. Miss DeFord had a very highly developed sense of family. That's always the surest sign of good breeding, don't you agree?"

He seemed to be waiting for my answer. I said, "Of course." Myrra was the daughter of an unskilled laborer and the ex-wife of a stevedore, but I didn't think he wanted to hear it.

"She also had a very highly developed sense of duty," Mr. Grandison said. "She aligned herself with causes. With very controversial causes, if I may say so. And there was her insistence on honesty, she had the highest standards of business honesty. Why, I've never seen anything like the fury of that remarkable woman when faced with even the slightest business indiscretion—"

"Mr. Grandison," I said, determined to get the conversation back to the present, "about the dog—"

"But I thought I explained it to you perfectly," he said. "I simply can't help you now. The procedures for the reading of a will have been established through centuries of custom. I cannot reveal the contents of Miss DeFord's last testament to you until Monday."

"Mr. Grandison," I said. "Please. I really don't want to know the contents of Myrra's will at this moment."

He looked shocked.

"But I don't understand," he said. "What do you want?"

I took the earring from the blotter, stroking Esmeralda in the process. She no longer looked panicked, but she did look forlorn.

"This earring," I said. "It belonged to Myrra and it must belong to someone now. And this dog. Do you have any idea what happened when Myrra died? What happened to the dog?"

"I don't understand," Mr. Grandison said. "Why are you concerned about a dog?"

"I'm concerned about what happened to this dog the night Myrra died," I said. "And I thought the earring was probably expensive. Myrra's jewelry usually was."

"You mean you didn't come about the apartment?" Mr. Grandison said. "You don't want to know the conditions you have to meet before you take over Miss DeFord's apartment?"

CHAPTER 8

"Do it again," Martinez said. "Start over again from the beginning."

I sighed and shut my eyes, trying to block out the white cinder-block room. I had been in Martinez's office for four hours. It was after eleven o'clock. I had missed my dinner. The only thing I wanted was to go home to bed, and I couldn't even do that. The police had sealed my apartment.

"On the night of December second, I was having a marathon," I repeated. "A marathon is when I write a whole romance book in five or six days. I was on the last day of one. I got up at ten or ten-thirty, made myself a cup of coffee, and sat down at the typewriter. I did not stop until dawn, when I went to sleep."

"You were alone the whole time?" Martinez said.

"Of course I was alone the whole time. I can't stand people around when I write. Even breathing distracts me."

"Did somebody call you?" Martinez said. "Did somebody visit?"

"If somebody called, they got the answering machine. Somebody probably did. If somebody rang the doorbell, they wouldn't have got an answer. But nobody rang the doorbell. Nobody rang the doorbell the entire five days."

Martinez sighed. "Isn't there any way you can corroborate any of this?"

"If you looked at the volume of work I produced that week—that month, for God's sake, I mean the month from November second to December second—even you'd think accusing me of running around murdering people was ludicrous. I cannot seem to get it into your head that fall is my busiest time. I get more than half the magazine work I do in a year between the middle of September and Christmas. In the past three months, I've written two romance novels, three major articles for national magazines, and no less than fifteen how-to columns on everything from handling a checking account to choosing a neurosurgeon. I didn't have *time* to murder anybody."

"I don't think that's going to go over," Martinez said. "You didn't kill Myrra Agenworth because you were too busy?"

"Oh, hell," I said, taking Camille out of my tote bag to let her play on Martinez's desk. "Ask Barbara. Maybe she heard me typing."

"Maybe," Martinez said. "Let's go over last night again."

I nearly exploded. "We've gone over it six times," I told him. "You've got the testimony of the cabdriver. You've got Phoebe's statement. Even you said the times were impossible."

"I said the times were tight."

"According to your own timetable, I had exactly six minutes between getting out of a cab in front of my apartment and waking Carlos to help me open the door. In those six minutes, I would have had to enter my apartment, stab a perfectly healthy woman nine times without anyone hearing a sound, walk out, figure a way to bolt the door from the outside, get Carlos, and start playing the injured innocent. Oh, come *on.*"

Martinez stared at the ceiling. The cat started climbing his tie.

"Earrings," he said. "Let's talk about earrings."

"What earrings?" Phoebe said. "*Whose* earrings?"

"Myrra's earrings." I leaned back to let the superannuated Greek waiter put a plate of shish kebab on the white Formica table. It was after midnight, and the Trio was the only restaurant in the neighborhood still serving dinner. The Trio was always serving dinner, and breakfast and lunch, twenty-four hours a day, seven days a week. It had linoleum on the floor and metal strips around the edges of the tables and a real soda fountain counter along one wall, but the food was very hot and very good and came in quantity. I preferred it to most of the smoked glass and polished chrome places that had opened on Columbus Avenue in the past year. I worried a little about the waiters, because they never seemed to go home. I had an almost irrepressible urge to ask Phoebe's Friend the Lawyer if Greeks ever got any sleep.

Phoebe's Friend the Lawyer was named Nicholas George Carras. He had very thick, very black, Kennedy-liberal long hair and blue eyes, a face straight out of a romance heroine's wet dream, and the kind of long, elegant fingers usually associated with safecrackers. He was also the tallest man I had ever seen outside professional basketball. He was taller than a lot of men *in* professional basketball.

If I hadn't been concentrating on killing Detective Martinez, I would have been ready to kill Phoebe.

"Myrra's earrings," I said, trying to drown out the sound of Nick's conversation (in Greek) with the waiter, "were missing from the body when it was found. Also the necklace. That ruby thing."

"They were supposed to go on exhibit at the conference," Phoebe said. "In a glass box. Jewels of Love."

"Jewels of Love." I put my head in my hands. Start at the beginning, I told myself. Things are coming apart. The small cat was at the bottom of my tote bag, shredding my American Express bill. Two people were dead. Phoebe had hired a lawyer on the basis of whether or not she would be able to marry me off to him. The police were holding Myrra's dog for vivisection.

I looked up into the eyes of Nick Carras. For the moment, he looked very intelligent. He had the eyes of a man who knew himself very well, and was amused, even when what he knew was not entirely to his credit. We exchanged smiles, because we both knew we were attracted to each other for superficial reasons. He was six eight at a minimum, and I liked men tall enough to make me feel small. I was a WASP from a moneyed family in Fairfield County, and there is something in every hyphenated American on the way up that wants me for a wife. Most of them can't distinguish one New England preppie from another. They make love to the concept instead of the woman, and end by feeling angry and betrayed by their children. Nick Carras, I thought, would not be one of those. I was beginning to like him very much.

"What I don't understand," he said, "is why the police think you killed this Agenworth woman. The Simms problem I can understand."

"I thought Myrra was mugged," Phoebe said, resentful.

"The apartment and the earrings," I said, still looking into Nick Carras's eyes. It's amazing how many minutes you can spend looking into someone else's eyes, especially if they're very blue, very deep, very intelligent eyes. "Myrra decided to leave me a little something in her will. Twelve rooms plus servants' wing in the Braedenvorst, plus everything in them at the time of her death."

"My God," Phoebe said. "That *apartment.*"

"Twelve rooms in the Braedenvorst," Nick said. "That must go for two or three million dollars." He looked shell-shocked. His theoretical rich girl had just turned into a very real heiress.

I couldn't stop myself from making it worse. "There are all those paintings," I said. "And the jewelry she kept lying around. Four original Degas. The contents of her wastebaskets. The heart-shaped bathtub."

"All right," Nick said. He had mastered his shock, but he was having trouble making things make sense. So was I, but I was used to confusion. It is not possible to live for long among romance writers without learning to think of insanity as background music.

Nick Carras thought of the world as both rational and explicable. He was trying.

"All right," he said again. "You and this Myrra Agenworth were good friends."

"Not exactly," I shook my head. This was what made it so difficult. "I would have said she was my friend, but I wasn't really hers. She adopted young women writers. I was one of them."

"Young women romance writers," Nick said.

"Not at all. I'm not really a romance writer. I started out doing investigative and women's rights pieces for the alternative press. Later I picked up a couple of the national slicks. It doesn't pay the rent. Romance pays the rent. Myrra got me into romance, and a lot of other people, too. Half the population of Manhattan Radical Feminists is now writing romance on the side."

"And pretending they aren't," Phoebe said. Her nose twitched. It was the only expression of contempt I'd ever seen her make. "They write four books a year for one of the lines and then run around saying how awful it is and romance should be prevented from taking up so much space in the bookstores. Caroline Hesse didn't even come to the funeral."

"Caroline Hesse has a Pulitzer Prize for journalism," Nick protested. "Magazine journalism."

"Caroline Hesse is Maura Sands for the Passion Romance line at Acme," Phoebe said. "None of them came to the funeral. There had to be dozens."

Nick turned to me. "You went to the funeral," he said. "You were closer to her than the others."

"Maybe." I toyed with a grilled green pepper. "I actually liked her, I guess. I wasn't just using her, and I think a lot of the people around her were. And I'm not ashamed of my Fires of Love books. They're silly, because the parameters of the genre as it now exists force them to be silly, but otherwise they're pretty good examples of the form. I can't afford to let anyone know I'm writing them, but it's not because I'm ashamed of them."

"Other people wouldn't understand," Nick suggested.

"Other people think it's the mark of the devil," I said.

"She thought you were wonderful," Phoebe said. "She thought you were a genius."

"If she did, I never heard about it."

"If she did, everybody else heard about it," Nick said. His air of purposefulness and conviction had returned, and he was sitting up straighter in his chair. I wondered what he had constructed to make my world comprehensible to him—and whether it would help or hurt me.

"They've got motive," he admitted. "But you have to have more than motive."

"He's got more than motive," I said. "He's got the earrings." I looked at the ceiling. This was no time to develop a crush on somebody's blue eyes. Things were much worse than Phoebe or Nick realized, much worse than I had ever expected them to be. Every time I thought of my last interview with Martinez, my throat felt as if it were being attacked by buzz saws.

"Myrra was wearing a pair of ruby earrings and a ruby necklace the night she was killed," I said. "They weren't on her when her body was found. One earring I say I found on Esmeralda's collar at the animal shelter. I'm the only one who noticed it there. The other earring—Well, they found the other earring in Julie's handbag, lying right there on the floor of my apartment after she was killed."

They were staring at me, shocked. I smiled like a woman close to death from seasickness.

"We know what Martinez thinks," I said. "Julie knew something about Myrra's death. Julie was trying to blackmail me or maybe just accuse me. Julie was found dead in my apartment."

CHAPTER 9

"Your picture's in the *Post*," Daniel said. "Did you see that? In the *Post*, for God's sake."

I cradled the phone between my shoulder and ear and reached across the bed to retrieve my cigarettes from Camille. We had a brief tug-of-war. She had captured my cigarettes and started a long trek to bury them in my tote bag. She did not appreciate my attempts to extract one for smoking purposes.

"Are you listening to me?" Daniel insisted. "You're not saying anything. I said your picture was in the goddamned New York *Post*."

I sighed. "I didn't think you read the *Post*," I said. "I thought it embarrassed you to be seen with it."

"I see the front page," he said. "I see the front page every time I pass a newsstand."

I got hold of a cigarette and lit it.

"All right," I told Daniel. "You saw my face on the front page of the New York *Post* while you were passing a newsstand. So what? Half the population of Manhattan saw my face on the front page of the *Post* while they were passing a newsstand."

"My point exactly," Daniel said. "Patience, there's a partnership vote on me in *three days.*"

"I thought those things were secret. I thought they never told you when—"

"Of course they don't tell you," he said. "You hear things. After eight years, I have quite a network for hearing things."

"I'm sure you do."

"And Patience," he said. "I took you to the firm dinner party last year. They all know you. I mean, they've all seen you, and once they see you—Well, Patience, you don't have the world's most *ordinary* looks. I mean, you've got to do something about this thing."

I told myself I should feel sympathetic. If for no other reason than that I had spent a great deal of my time during the last few years nursing Daniel's hopes, dreams, and fears about partnership, I should bleed for him now. I couldn't.

"Listen," I told him. "I'm very sorry for all your embarrassment." Was I really saying this? "I hope nothing goes wrong with the partnership. But Daniel, I just don't see what I can do about it."

"Are you trying to tell me you can't tell the police where you were when that woman got killed? Are you saying they've got a *case?*"

"Since nobody knows when that woman got killed, as you put it, I don't see how I could convince them I wasn't there."

"Oh, Jesus," Daniel said. "You were there. This thing is going to trial."

"Sometime, someplace, this thing is going to trial," I agreed.

"Oh, Jesus," Daniel said again.

Then he hung up.

I put the receiver into the cradle and looked around the large, baroque/modern bedroom for my robe. The bedroom was in a suite at the Cathay-Pierce. Phoebe always rented a suite at the Cathay-Pierce for the conference, even though her apartment was just across the Park, because she wanted "to be around to do business," meaning go to parties.

I found my robe and started to get out of bed to put it on. The phone rang again.

"Phoebe?" The woman on the other end of the line had a very heavy accent.

"Phoebe's in the next room," I said. "I'll get her."

"You tell Nick," the woman said. "He left the house, he didn't take his orange pills. You tell him."

The phone went dead.

I put on my robe, put Camille in my pocket, and went into the sitting room of the suite. Nick and Phoebe were sitting together on the couch, looking like the bomb had fallen. I took a cheese Danish from the room service tray and sat on the floor.

"You forgot your orange pills," I told Nick. "Some woman called and told me to tell you."

"Vitamin C," Nick said. "My mother. She's up visiting from New Jersey."

I put Camille on the floor to play.

"Daniel thinks I did it," I told Phoebe. "Can you believe that? He's known me for three years and he thinks I did it."

"Which?" Nick Carras said.

"Both, I guess. We were talking about Julie."

"Daniel Harte." Phoebe made a sound like an angry horse. "Daniel Harte would believe anything. What did he call for, anyway? You're embarrassing him?"

"Something like that." I lay down on the floor and let Camille climb onto my stomach. She began making her way to my pockets. "The way this thing is going," I said, trying to make myself sound as reasonable as possible, "the only way we're going to convince Martinez I didn't murder two people is to let him know who did. I mean—"

"Don't even think about it," Nick said. He got off the couch and started pacing, his long legs jerking arrhythmically. "I've been through this before," he said. "I used to work for Nader. You know what happens when an interested party starts investigating for itself? It gets in deeper. It ends up at all the wrong places at all the wrong times. Look what happened when you went out to the animal shelter."

"I didn't go out to the animal shelter to investigate," I said. "I went to get a cat." I sat up. "Were you really with Nader?" I asked. "I'm impressed."

"Washington office," Nick said. "Three years. My point is that you're in all the wrong places at all the wrong times as it is. All we need is to have you wandering into another murder, or finding the knife—"

"And I've seen all those books in your bag," Phoebe said. "Life is not Hercule Poirot. You're not going to find out how to solve this thing by reading the complete works of Arthur Conan Doyle."

"Dorothy L. Sayers," I said. My hair was falling into my face, and I hefted it aside. "I was just getting myself acclimatized. And you've got to admit this thing looks like an Agatha Christie. And Martinez could probably get an indictment right now if he wanted to. God only knows what he's waiting for."

"He's not." Nick leaned over and shoved his face into mine. His blue eyes had dark flecks in them but no dreams. To him, this situation was a reality he neither could nor wanted to escape. I resented it. It was easier for me to imagine myself the heroine of a thirties murder mystery, where all the moves were planned in advance to reveal a true killer. I faced his calm examination of strategies with distaste. He went on.

"According to my friend in the district attorney's office, you're shortly to have a date with a grand jury."

"Oh, fine."

"And as things stand now," Nick sat down on the couch beside Phoebe, "you're going to be indicted, and you're going to go to trial. You can't afford to mess around in this thing."

"I can't afford *not* to." Now I was up and pacing. Camille was jouncing around in my pocket like a baby kangaroo. "Don't you realize what's going on? This thing is *crazy*. Muggers who return earrings. Locked rooms. Dogs tied up at the animal shelter. What was Julie doing in my apartment in the first place, can you tell me that? She's never been to my apartment. I don't think she knew where I lived."

"That's our selling point," Nick said, suddenly sounding all briskly professional. "How did that door get locked? If we can get the jury thinking about how that door got locked . . ."

"Not *how*," I insisted. "*Why*. Why in God's name go to all that trouble? I mean, okay. Maybe somebody knew Barbara had a key and they didn't want her finding the body, they wanted me to find the body. But why me? Why not kill Julie in Central Park? My apartment isn't *convenient* to anything."

"That's an idea," Nick said. "Who knew this Barbara had a key to your apartment?"

"Half the island of Manhattan," Phoebe said. "She's always telling Barbara stories."

"And how did they get into my apartment in the first place? The police said the lock wasn't forced. They could be wrong, since they kicked the door in, but *still.* " I stopped for breath. "I know this is going to sound crazy," I said, "but I'm beginning to think I've been set up."

I looked at the two of them, sitting side by side on the couch. They weren't going to be any help. I might be able to talk Phoebe into something later, but for the moment I was on my own.

I tightened the belt of my robe and started toward the bedroom.

"I've got to get dressed," I said. "I've got First Novel at ten-thirty."

"Just a minute," Phoebe said. From the way the two of them were looking at each other, I knew there was something very wrong. I waited in the bedroom door.

"I wasn't going to tell you this," Phoebe said. "But they found Myrra's necklace, the one she was wearing? It arrived in the mail this morning, in a brown manila envelope, addressed to 'Chairman, Jewels of Love Committee.' I think Amelia opened it."

CHAPTER 10

I met Hazel Ganz going down in the elevator. I was too preoccupied to notice her at first—I was involved in an elaborate fantasy in which Amelia Samson sent her wrens like a flock of miniaturized pterodactyls to murder her best friend and her agent—but Hazel planted herself in front of me soon enough.

"They're killing us," she told me. "They're *killing* us."

"Who?" I took her literally.

"Editors." Hazel waved vaguely at the elevator doors. *"Publishers.* Ninety titles a month this year. A hundred and eighty next year. How long do you think that's going to last?"

"Oh well," I said. "They've been talking about a market shakeout for the past two years. It hasn't happened yet."

"It will. What's going to happen to us then? I've got two kids. I want to send them to college. I'm not ready to go back to getting chased around the instrument tray by Dr. Harold Shenshorn, D.D.S."

"I don't blame you," I murmured.

"What would you know about it? Did you ever have to be a dental assistant? Of course not. Did you ever worry about where the money was coming from? Don't be ridiculous. Just look at you." The elevator doors opened on the lobby floor. "Fires of Love is going to fold," Hazel Ganz said. "It's got no guts."

I waited until she disappeared into the opposite bank of elevators, the ones for the West Tower. Then I wandered across the lobby to the glass-enclosed, black-and-white plastic Calender of Events, wondering if I really believed that Amelia's flock of sharp-beaked wrens had murdered two people. I decided it was as good an explanation as any. The wrens seemed too timid to me, but Lydia Wentward seemed too drugged out, Janine Williams too fastidious, and Phoebe too solidly alibied (by me). Mary Allard was a distinct possibility, but I didn't like the woman. If there was one thing I had learned from my intensive late-night reading of *The Murder of Roger Ackroyd*, it was that the murderer was unlikely to be the character you liked least.

I had located the room for the Charlotte/First Novel Category meeting (Charlotte Brontë Award/Best First Novel in Paperback Category Romance), when I felt a tap on my shoulder and heard a high-pitched throat-clearing death rattle behind me. I turned and looked right into the faces of two escapees from *Pink Flamingos*.

There was a tall one and a short one. The tall one was very thin, with dyed blacker-than-black wiry hair to her shoulders, dead white foundation all over her face, and heavy rouge on both her cheeks and lips. The short one was very round, with straw blond hair tortured into two tiny mouse-ear pigtails. Both of them were smiling at me.

"Are you Jeri Andrews?" the tall one said. Her head wobbled back and forth as if it wasn't tightly anchored on her neck.

"I'm both Jeri Andrews and Andrea Nicholas." I worked to bring a smile to my face. If there is a commandment in romance writing, it is Honor Thy Fan. Everybody obeys it. Editors solicit and act upon the opinions of their readers about the future direction of their lines. Marketing directors throw reader parties in obscure cities, complete with free champagne and author appearances. Authors allow *Romantic Times* to publish the details of their private lives. There are no Emily Dickinsons or Thomas Pynchons in romance. The fans would never allow it.

These two were not only fans, but aspirants. They were both wearing blue heart-shaped badges marked "writer," which is what the American Writers of Romance likes to call unpublished novelists. Published novelists are called "authors."

"We thought so," the short one said. She stared at me the way Lydia does when she's put too much powder up her nose, but I didn't think this woman's problem was drugs. The idea that she was naturally this *disconnected* made me uneasy. It didn't help that she was dressed in a white concoction of ribbons and bows, and wearing a white rose in her hair with a stem long enough to run through her teeth.

"It's about Miss Simms," the short one said. "The agent? The one who died?" She reached into her handbag, pulled out a fat, battered envelope, and thrust it into my stomach. "She said we were to give it to you. She called you some name—"

"Who did?"

"Miss Simms," the tall one said. "She was going to be my agent. She read my novel and just *loved* it. She said I was very clear. Every time my character thought about something, I was always careful to put 'she was thinking' right there on the page."

"Last Wednesday," the short one said. "We went to Miss Simms's office to pick up some material for Gamble here—"

"Gamble Daere," the tall one said. "I thought it sounded distinctive. I didn't want to have one of those names that sounded like all the other names."

"The thing is," the short one said, "it wasn't material for Gamble. And when we opened it we found—" She blushed a deep, bright red. "Well, it's private and it's personal and it's none of my business, if you ask me. So you take it. She told us to give it to you."

"But you never would have thought it," Gamble Daere said. "It just goes to show you you never know."

"When did Julie tell you to give me this?" I asked. "She *died* Thursday."

"She died Thursday night," the short one said. "We talked to her Thursday morning. Thing is, we live upstate—"

"In Goshen," the tall one said.

"So we couldn't come down to her office and give it to her, not right away. So we called and asked if she wanted us to mail it to her, but she said definitely *not*. So we were bringing it to the funeral. She told us to look for you. She told us if we couldn't find her at the funeral, we should look for a very tall, very blond woman probably dressed in pants."

"They wouldn't let us in," the tall one sniffed. "We had to stand on the steps, and then not very far up the steps. There was a big line that went all around the block, and they kept us out there in the cold."

The short one threw the tall one a look of long-suffering exasperation. Then she thrust the envelope into my stomach again.

"You take this," she said. "We were supposed to deliver it to Miss Simms or give it to you to give to her. I don't know what you're going to do with it now she's dead, but I don't want the responsibility for it anymore."

"I don't know what I'm going to do now she's dead, either," the tall one said. "Miss Simms was one of the few people in publishing willing to look beyond personal prejudice at real talent." She fixed me with a knowing glare. "Everybody around here has friends," she said ominously.

The short one pulled at the tall one's beribboned sleeve. "We won't bother you anymore," she said, trying to push Gamble Daere into the background. "You take that and do what you think best with it."

CHAPTER 11

"Oh God," Janine said. "I'm sorry. I should have realized what was going on, but I was so caught up in that Allard woman's nonsense, I was not on this planet. They didn't destroy you, did they, dear?"

She stabbed her finger at the elevator button, managing to look worried and hurried at once. She also looked pleased, cat-swallowed-the-canary pleased, safe behind her wall of Belonging. She was like this whenever she met "outsiders," no matter how often it happened over how long a period of time. It was as if her job as a romance editor was the equivalent of a position on the high school cheerleading squad. The mere fact of it guaranteed Difference. She could not be mistaken for one of the poor mortals out there.

I turned away from her and said, "Just a couple of fans. No problem."

"Looks like they stuck you with a proposal." She pointed to the envelope I was holding. I turned it over in my hand and then stuck it out of sight in my tote bag.

"Something like that," I said. "I don't mind." I wanted to make a dash for the nearest ladies room to look the thing through in private, but I didn't dare. Whatever Julie Simms wanted badly enough to give those two women a second interview would have to wait until I had a chance to lock myself in Phoebe's suite. What Julie *intended* to give them was no mystery. She had a standard "information kit for romance writers," a formidable, pessimistic overview of the genre meant to scare the worst of them into some other line of work.

The elevator doors slid open and we stepped inside.

"What's Mary doing to you now?" I asked Janine.

"She's not doing it to *me*," Janine said. "I've protested of course, but anyone would. What she's done is gone to the Organizing Committee and claimed Julie was proposing her as her second for the Line Committee."

"But Julie couldn't stand the woman," I said. The Line Committee translated as the Charlotte Brontë Award for Best Category Romance Line of the Year, and it was the most important committee at the conference. The winning line was allowed to display the picture of the little gold statue of Charlotte Brontë on all its books and in all its television advertising for the next year. Janine's Fires of Love line had been nominated, as had Dell's Candlelight Ecstasy and Simon and Schuster's Silhouette Desire. These were the sexiest lines in the business, the ones old-time romance writers raged about when they accused "all those new people" of perpetrating "soft-core porn." They weren't soft-core porn, but they had more good parts per square inch than anything but.

"I'm not saying anyone's taking her seriously," Janine said. "No one wants her on the committee anyway. But it seems she has a letter from Julie, saying that if anything happens to Julie Simms . . . Well, you see what I mean."

"Julie Simms wrote a letter telling the Organizing Committee what to do *in case anything happened to her?*"

Janine shrugged. "We're going to have to turn it over to the police, of course. They've been crawling all over here since Thursday, and now it's going to be worse."

"It's a little strange," I said. "It sounds as if—"

"Oh, I know," Janine said. "It sounds as if she knew she was going to die. But of course, that's ridiculous. She was probably worried she'd get sick, and she wanted to be sure whoever took her place on the committee would do what she wanted. I suppose she thought Mary would be so grateful to be taken back into the fold, she'd have complete loyalty. Although how Julie could think something like that is beyond me."

"She wouldn't," I said. "Mary Allard wouldn't know loyalty from a hole in the wall."

"That's exactly what the rest of us think," Janine said. "And we don't know what we're going to do with her this evening, because we've already picked Julie's replacement. Not that I'm on the committee, of course, but they did ask me about you when your name came up, and—"

"I'm supposed to be sitting in Julie's place on the *Line* Committee?"

Janine stared at the floor and fidgeted. "Well," she said. "We all thought . . . it did seem, since the police insisted on harping on this ridiculous theory . . . we knew you couldn't—"

"A kind of vote of confidence," I suggested, wishing the people with my "best interests at heart" would leave me alone. One of the things that goes along with being a member of the Line Committee is an all-out attack by the editors in chief. Romance novels by the gross arrive in one's mailbox. Posters of half-naked men and women staring intently into each other's eyes pile up like copies of the Sunday *Times* during a sanitation workers' strike. Steel-eyed clones of Sandra Dee corner you in restaurants and give speeches about the Necessity for Fairness and Objectivity, which will lead you to vote for . . .

"We thought it would be perfectly clear to everyone that we didn't think you had anything to do with Julie's death if we put you on the Line Committee," Janine said. "And besides, you really are the best person for the job. I mean, it can't be an editor with a line up for the award, and it can't be Lydia, because Lydia has been flying since Myrra's funeral. *So.*"

"Right," I said.

"Don't worry about anything," Janine said. "You just come down to the meeting tonight and see what happens with Mary. If we *have* to honor her letter, we will, but then we'll put you in Julie's place on the Individual Series."

The elevator doors slid open on seventeen and she stepped out. They were about to shut again when my hand shot out and caught them.

"Just a minute." I blushed. I knew what I wanted to ask, but I didn't know why I wanted to ask it. Janine was poised just outside the elevator door, looking studiedly curious. "It was something Hazel Ganz said," I stammered. "About Fires of Love. And market shakeouts—"

"Oh, that." Janine scratched the side of her nose. "We had a little trouble after Romantic Life. I mean, the first couple of months for Fires of Love—" She shrugged her shoulders. "I took care of *that*," she said. "If there's a market shakeout, we're going to be the only line left. There's never been anything like Fires of Love."

"Right," I said.

"Let *me* worry about that sort of thing," she said. She gave me a little wave. "Back to the computers."

If I was a *real* romance writer, like Phoebe, I would have put that "she said gaily."

CHAPTER 12

"Number eighteen. Passion's Whisper by Leyla Johns."

"Oh God."

"That's the one that takes place entirely in a sauna. After they've spent two solid weeks together in this sauna—I'm not kidding, they don't do anything else—he makes his move and she faints."

"And the hero's name is Bryce Cannon. I'm not sure if she was misreading the news when she wrote it, or if she's got some weird Freudian thing about guns."

"Listen to this: 'Amelia heard the knock on her door and jumped, startled, to her feet. Telling herself to have courage, she concentrated on the sound of her steel-sharp heels as they crossed the red, blue, and gold mosaic of the entry-foyer floor, heading for the oaken door.'"

"Oh God."

"Can't we just discard the ones we know are impossible? We've got a hundred and twenty-two titles on that list."

"What is that thing, anyway, a gothic?"

"Number nineteen. Flame of Desire, by Marianna Brand."

"Oh please."

I took the only empty seat at the table and looked over Hazel Ganz's shoulder to see what was going on. Nineteen entries, nineteen "certainly nots" penciled into the margin of her voting card. Hazel looked fierce, fierce and disgusted and ready to give it all up for a life of professional assassination.

"Where do you stand on pseudonyms?" she asked, turning around in her chair to avoid the sight of *Flame of Desire*, a Fires of Love Book with a painting of a half-naked blonde with breasts three times too large for her frame being helped into a back bend by a tall, dark stranger on the cover.

"What do you mean?"

"You have to write under a pseudonym, right? And the company owns your pseudonym, so you can't take it with you, right? I mean, if the publisher treats you like dirt, and you want to go to another company, you can't take your pseudonym with you. So you aren't anybody. You've got no *leverage.*"

"Right," I said. "Romance writers should own their pseudonyms."

"Romance writers should write under their own names," Hazel said. "They can't copyright your real name. Would John Irving write under a pseudonym? Would Norman Mailer? The way it is with us, we can't build up any *equity.* They can do anything they want to us. They *do* anything they want to us."

The chairman rapped her gavel for attention. I took advantage of the lull to grab a handful of heart-shaped valentine candies from the bowl in front of me. They were the kind with messages printed on them that turned to sand in your teeth.

"Please," the chairman said. "We're on number nineteen. Can we vote on number nineteen?"

" 'Oh, Roger, how can you believe I'm *that* kind of woman?' " someone squeaked.

"Please," the chairman said. "This is just a nomination list. We have to have a nomination list for the cocktail party Sunday night. That's *tomorrow,* people."

"We ought to restrict the damn list to four," someone said.

"Then we'd never get out of here," someone else said.

"Number twenty," the chairman said. *"Jewel of Desire,* by Anastasia Smythe."

"Listen to this." Hazel Ganz was on her feet, waving the book in the air. " '*She felt the hard line of his muscular thighs as he pressed against her. His breath was hot and ragged in her ears as his hands roved over every inch of her body, probing her depths.*' "

"My God," the chairman said. "That's practically pornography."

"It's the direction we should be going in," Hazel Ganz insisted.

"We've already put two pieces of absolute crap on this list, for ridiculously sentimental reasons, which is exactly what all those people out there sneer at us for. We ought to put at least one title on the list that's an example of the best romance can do."

I didn't think the best romance could do would ever appear in a category line. The publishers are afraid of losing the "instant identification" that makes them so much money, so author's guidelines are too detailed, and formulas are too rigid. What results is usually an unsurprising mix of drivel and sentimentality, buoyed up by lengthy descriptions of the exact path his manhood travels to the core of her womanhood.

I knew a full-scale filibuster when I heard one, however. I sank in my chair, prepared to eat my way through valentine candies until it was over. I reached into my tote bag for my cigarettes and came out instead with Camille and the white envelope I'd picked up in the lobby. They came out together because Camille was chewing the envelope, having already destroyed the computer card for the payment of my electric bill. I decided this was basically my fault (would you like to be left at the bottom of a tote bag for half an hour?) and put both Camille and her toy on the table. Then I found my cigarettes and lit one, resolutely ignoring the disapproving glare of the little girl in pink and green makeup on my right. By then, Camille had given up the envelope and begun worrying the dish of valentine candies.

I picked up the white envelope and started to draw out the papers inside, a thick sheaf, some folded, some loose. At the back was a pack of snapshots, the bled-to-the-edges kind typical of those one-day developing services in supermarket parking lots. Most of them were both murky and boring, having been taken in a restaurant somewhere under conditions of minimal light. There was Amelia Samson with a woman who looked like one of her wrens, eating alone at a table for four. Amelia had some kind of fowl, two baked potatoes dripping sour cream and chives, a large dinner roll, asparagus with hollandaise sauce, and a brandy snifter full of wine. The wren had a chef's salad.

I went through a few more pictures of restaurant scenes, all different, then came to three photographs of what looked like completely blank

pieces of white paper. It was almost possible to see the shape of the
overhead lamp from the points of brilliance on the film. I turned the
last of these pictures over and over and upside down. I couldn't make
sense of it. I flipped it to the back of the pack and looked down at the
next to the last print.

And very nearly vomited then and there.

My nausea lasted just long enough for the fear to settle into my arms
and neck. In less than a minute, I was too stiff to move, convinced for
some crazy reason that if I called attention to myself I would also call
attention to the photograph. It didn't matter that the picture was
hidden from the woman on my right by my tote bag, which I'd put on
the table to act as a barrier for the cigarette smoke, and that Hazel
Ganz, standing up, was too far out of range to make anything out in
the muddy print.

It didn't help to put the picture at the back of the pack, because
there was another one. I put that one back, too, then put the whole
pack into the envelope. There was another set of smaller prints, stuck
at the bottom in a corner, but I didn't want to look at them. There was
also a set of papers. I tried to steady myself.

The nausea finally passed. As my head cleared, I began to realize I
had the one thing even Martinez had not been able to unearth: a
motive for the murder of Julie Simms. Martinez might want to believe
I had killed Myrra for her money and Julie because she'd found out
about Myrra, but there were holes in that theory and even he knew it.
For one thing, until the murder of Julie Simms, Myrra's death had
been officially accepted as a mugging. Why would I, or anyone else,
commit a second murder to cover an adequately covered first?

What was in that envelope, however, had no holes in it. What was
in that envelope would have roughly the same effect on one career and
two reputations as the Allied bombing had had on Dresden.

I reached into the envelope and pulled out the papers. Then, feeling
the paranoia creep under my skin like a hot pin, I shielded myself from
the rest of the table with my tote bag and sweater. The little girl in
pink and green makeup asked if I was hot, but I ignored her.

The large, folded papers were photostats, mainly of hotel registers in places like Northfield, Vermont, and Mystic, Connecticut. By themselves they didn't mean anything. Neither did the two letters, written in Amelia's spidery script on stiff, inscribed stationery from Cartier's, although they were suggestive. Suggestive merely, they didn't count. If I had found them, I wouldn't have jumped to conclusions, although somebody had.

The loose papers were checking account deposit slips, preencoded to Amelia's account in the New York Guaranty Trust. Each was made out for one thousand dollars cash, and each was dated the first, second, or third of succeeding months. There were twelve of them in all. January first, February first, March first, on through the coming year.

I looked at them over and over again in confusion. It didn't make sense. The obvious explanation was that someone (Julie Simms?) was blackmailing Amelia over these photographs. But the money was going *into* Amelia's account, not out of it. It didn't add up.

I put the deposit slips in a pile and back into the envelope. A woman Phoebe and I had known in college worked for the New York Guaranty. As soon as I had a chance, I'd call her.

I turned my attention to the photographs. Now that I knew what I was looking for, the woman with the chef's salad no longer looked like a wren. I flipped through the restaurant scenes and came to the blank white prints, which now seemed to be sales slips of some sort. Then I passed on to the two prints at the end. This time, what I saw was less shocking than sad. Two women, engaged in something it must have been very difficult for them to start and even more difficult for them to continue. Two women, growing old, growing tired, growing lonely, looking for a substitute for something they had once found both necessary and unpleasant. Two women, forced by the cruelties of nature and age into positions so aesthetically unsuitable they could only be disgusting.

Amelia and Myrra.

CHAPTER 13

"You're out of your *mind*," Marian Pinckney said. "Do you have the faintest idea what you're asking me to do? I can't just go poking around in someone's account records because you found a bunch of deposit slips."

"Marian," I said. "We've been through this before. It's not just a bunch of deposit slips." I turned my back on Nick, who was pressing his face against the glass of the telephone booth door and making fish faces at me. I had been in the booth for an hour. He had been trying to get me out of it for the last thirty minutes. "Listen," I told Marian. "You have the right to investigate what you think may be a crime, don't you?"

"I have no evidence of a crime," Marian said. "And neither do you."

"I've got photographs of two people in a very compromising position," I recited. "I've got photographs of incriminating documents. I've got a purloined love letter—"

"Nobody gives a shit about affairs anymore," Marian said. "How did you get in touch with me, anyway? My number isn't listed."

"I called Sharon Hewitt."

"In *Kansas?*"

"Kansas City, Missouri."

"My God. How's she doing, anyway? I told her when she married that idiot she'd be miserable, and she probably is. Kansas City, Missouri. Yuck. Cows. And besides, she doesn't have this number."

"She had Tania Griswald's number, and Tania had yours."

"Tania Griswald lives in the British West Indies."

"I know."

"Oh Christ." Sound of a match, heavy breathing, quick whistling exhale. "I suppose that means you're serious," she said. "Calling the British West Indies. Jesus H. Christ."

"For God's sake, Marian, if I didn't know you graduated Phi Bete, I'd think you were a complete idiot. Now will you listen to me? I'm sitting here with an envelope with a lot of dirty pictures in it, and hotel records, and love letters, and a full dozen deposit slips each made out to the first of the month and each for one thousand dollars cash, and if that doesn't sound like blackmail to you, I don't know what would."

"Wait," Marian said. "Back up. What did you say? A thousand dollars a month?"

"Cash."

"Always the first of the month."

"The first or the second or the third. I figure it's allowing for weekends."

"Weekends," Marian said. "I didn't think of weekends. We have EFT."

"What are you talking about?"

"Never mind," she said. "Just hold on. Just stay on the phone and don't hang up. I'll be back in a minute."

She put the hold button on, and a very tinny band began playing "MacArthur Park" in my ear. I put the phone against my shoulder, extracted a cigarette from the pack in my pocket, and retrieved Camille from the tote bag. Nick was still leaning against the booth door. He was beginning to look angry.

I turned my back to him again. I was going to have to tell him all about this, and after I calmed him down, I was going to have to convince him to help. I sneaked a look at him over my shoulder. It was an oddly exciting thought, working side by side with a common purpose . . .

Just like a romance novel.

I took a very deep drag on my cigarette. Neither Miss Marple nor Hercule Poirot allowed sexual impulsiveness to get in the way of an investigation. Especially when the impulse seemed to arise from nothing but . . . aesthetics.

The music clicked off. "Marian?" I said. "Are you there?"

Inhale. Sharp whistle exhale. Small snort. "Oh, I'm here," she said. "Now, what name did you say this account is supposed to be in?"

"I didn't say," I said. "But it's Amelia Samson."

"Amelia Samson the writer? Virgins in love, that one?"

"Right."

"Shit. Fine. Tremendous. What's the account number?"

I read it off to her.

"Damn," Marian said. "Double goddamn."

"What's the matter?" I asked her, so excited I could hardly take a decent drag on my cigarette. "Do you have something on that account? Do you know something about Amelia?"

"The only thing I know about Amelia Samson," Marian said, "is that on the basis of her prose, she'd have failed English Ia at Greyson. And no, I don't have anything on her account. I've never heard of her account."

"I don't understand," I said, deflated. "You sounded so excited. Like you *knew* something."

"I don't know a thing," Marian said. "But I ought to. Oh boy, how I ought to. This thing is so screwy—"

"There's something I ought to tell you," I said. "This thing *is* screwy. I mean—"

"Do you know," Marian said, "I'm the only senior vice president in charge of operations in any bank in the entire world who happens to be female? Do you know what that *means*? Do you know what a responsibility that is? If this thing is what I think it is, they're every last one of them going to say it only happened at New York Guaranty because New York Guaranty was fool enough to put a woman in charge of operations. Just you wait."

"Well, before you go charging off, listen to me," I said. "It's not as easy as you think. I'm sure this is blackmail, but I don't know who's blackmailing who. Amelia Samson is the one in the pictures, and she should be the one getting blackmailed, but the account—"

"No problem," Marian said. "I know how *that* works." She didn't explain. "Where are you going to be tonight? Say, after nine?"

I thought about it. The Line Committee meeting was set for eight-thirty.

"I've got a working dinner and a meeting," I said. "I know I'll be in by eleven." I gave her the number. "That's a suite at the Cathay-Pierce. If you lose the number, ask for Miss Damereaux."

"Damereaux," Marian said. "Right. You're as screwy as you ever were. Listen, I've got to go put this thing in the computer. I'll call you later and tell you what I know."

"All right," I said.

"At eleven," Marian said.

"I'll be here."

"I still think Sharon has to be miserable among the cows," Marian said. "Cows, for God's sake. Whoever heard of anyone being happy about the cows?"

She hung up before I could explain that Kansas City was a fair-sized urban district without any (or many) cows. At least, I didn't think it had cows.

The booth door jammed open. Nick leaned in, picked up Camille, and dropped a piece of baklava in my hand.

"I give up," he said. "Just tell me *who's* blackmailing you."

CHAPTER 14

"If I tell you to stop," Nick said, "you're not going to listen to me."

"No."

The waitress brought a shot of Jack Daniel's on a black plastic tray. Nick took it and poured it into my coffee. We were in the Castle Walk Lounge, a bar on the ground floor of the Cathay-Pierce priced for tourists and expense accounts, at a table in a window looking out on Fifth Avenue. On the street, fifty-year-old women in overpriced clothes posed at lampposts, frozen for attention.

"Drink your coffee," Nick said. "You're still shaking."

I took a deep gulp of something that tasted like mocha medicine and put the cup back into the saucer. Outside it was getting dark, sliding into that gray half-light of New York City winters that made most of any day feel like an infinitely extended evening. We had called Phoebe, and she was coming down. It should have been a quiet time.

If I put my hands on the coffee cup, the liquid inside jerked and waved, my fingers rattled against the glass. Nick sat in a shadow, his face obscured, his voice like God setting down the commandments, his history impossible to untangle. Phoebe said she had known him when she was growing up. Union City, New Jersey. He had gone to Harvard and been a year ahead of Daniel at the Harvard Law School. He had been in the Army and in Vietnam, but not for long. He had been a Nader's Raider. Phoebe gave lists, not explanations.

The lists did not explain what I was feeling. Neither did his manner. He just seemed like a very comfortable man.

I stopped Camille in the process of burying one of the hotel's best napkin rings in my tote bag.

"This is getting to be a habit," I said. "She steals things and hides them in my bag."

"Why don't you tell me what's wrong?" Nick said. "If you want to wait for Phoebe, we can wait for Phoebe."

"I don't want to wait for Phoebe," I said. "And the real problem is that I don't know what's wrong. I just know something is." I put Camille in the tote bag and hoped she'd stay there. "We've got Myrra dead and Julie dead," I told him. "I think everybody knows the two deaths are connected by now. And we've got this envelope. According to the people who gave it to me, Julie had the envelope. So that must be connected. But you tell me, Nick. *How* are they connected?"

Nick shrugged. "Amelia was blackmailing Myrra. Myrra threatened to expose her. Amelia killed Myrra. Julie found out about it. Amelia killed Julie."

"In my apartment."

"Amelia knew you stood to inherit the apartment."

"No possible way," I shook my head. "Nobody knew I stood to inherit that apartment but Myrra and her lawyers. I don't care what kind of relationship Myrra had with Amelia. She wouldn't have revealed the contents of that will to anyone." I sighed. "You didn't know Myrra," I told him. "I did. That has to be one of my biggest problems."

"At the moment, your biggest problem is a grand jury indictment for second-degree murder."

I waved it away. "Consider the blackmail," I said. "I don't care what Myrra had done, if somebody had tried to blackmail her, she'd have exploded all over three continents. Myrra had absolutely no morality when it came to sex, but she was a hell and damnation fanatic when it came to money. If somebody had tried to blackmail Myrra, she'd have called the police or she'd have killed him. She wouldn't have paid it."

"Doesn't that prove my point?"

"No. If she'd known Amelia was being blackmailed, she wouldn't have let Amelia pay it. And let's face it. If they weren't blackmailing each other, somebody had to be blackmailing both of them."

"Myrra blackmails Amelia," Nick said. "Amelia kills her for it. Julie finds out about it. Amelia kills Julie."

"What would Myrra want to blackmail Amelia for? Myrra had to be worth twenty million dollars."

"Twenty-six." Phoebe slid into the booth beside Nick. Her velvet caftan was scarlet. Her eyes looked like deep black lakes set in gray and aquamarine deserts. She beamed at the two of us. We had been alone, together, talking. Love, marriage, and a house in Westchester would inevitably follow. "Someone named Barbara Gilbert called," she said. "Is that Barbara from next door? She sounded *hysterical.*"

I pushed the envelope to her. She looked inside, paled slightly, and put it down. She didn't look surprised.

"I don't see how people can stand to take pictures of this kind of thing."

"You're not shocked," Nick said.

"About Amelia and Myrra?" Phoebe put her tiny hands in her hair. "I thought that was what you meant on the phone. But it's not that strange, is it? They were very close. Every close friendship has a sexual basis."

"My God," Nick said.

Phoebe smiled at us like a ten-year-old child taking bows at her first piano recital. She was perfectly serious.

"This Barbara person said there was someone lurking around your apartment," Phoebe said. "Someone who looked like Ben Hur. Actually, what she said was, it *was* Ben Hur. But of course I knew she must mean *looked like*—"

"It's probably a policeman," I said. "If there's anyone there at all. Barbara is always seeing someone lurking."

"It's not a policeman," Phoebe said. "He got into the building and was hanging around right outside your door until she called the super and had him put out. And that's when she got really hysterical. On the phone, I mean. The super put the man out, and he fell on the sidewalk and couldn't get up. And he kept yelling something about not having very much time, and it was awful. I think."

"It's cold," I said. "Probably some drunk off the street." I picked up the envelope and turned it over and over in my hands. Nick was still in the shadows, but he was watching me. I had a nearly irresistible urge to brush my hair.

Or eat.

Left to myself, I don't care much about my hair and I tend to starve myself on general principles.

"What are we going to do about this?" I asked.

"What can we do about it?" Nick said. "Wait till your friend at the bank gets back to us."

"Don't be ridiculous," Phoebe said. "We'll go up and talk to Amelia. She's having a tea. Because of the campaign." Nick blinked, and she explained. "Amelia's running for President of the Association," she said. "Against Lydia."

CHAPTER 15

"Lydia Wentward," Amelia Samson said, "is a pornographer."

I had half a mind to tell her she looked like a transvestite. She sat in pompadoured splendor, flanked on either side by wrens. Her hair was piled into a lacquered mountain of strawberry blond curls. Her silver-gray dress, made of heavy brocade, was cut nearly to her navel. Her breasts, which made Dolly Parton's look flat, were concealed by an ornate, yellow-gold breastplate sprinkled with rhinestones and ending in a choke collar disturbingly similar to the one on Amanuensis, her Siamese cat. Beside her, the wrens were dressed in brown cotton shirt-waists, each with a tiny barrette of baby's breath and lilac in her hair, each with her legs crossed at the ankles. When Amelia said "pornographer," they each looked painfully shocked and giggled.

"What about you?" Amelia looked at me. "Don't you think Lydia Wentward is a pornographer?"

"I don't know," I said. "I've never read any of her books. I've read Phoebe's books, and they don't necessarily close at the bedroom door."

"Nonsense," Amelia said. "There's no comparison. Phoebe handles her love scenes with discretion and taste."

Phoebe beamed. Nick and I shot her a disbelieving look. Phoebe's love scenes were famous for being not only "poetic," but more complicated than the most esoteric positions in *More Joy of Sex*.

"The problem with Lydia," Amelia was going on, "is that she doesn't take her work seriously. She cares about nothing but money. She doesn't realize what a responsibility we have to the women of this country." She picked her teacup up in two ringed fingers, her pinkie, adorned with a small garnet and a very large amethyst, held defiantly in the air. "Bodice rippers," she said venomously. "Rape fantasies."

"Maybe that's why Julie wouldn't handle some of her work," Phoebe said, trying to look helpful and innocent. "There was a novel a few years ago—"

"Savage Breath of Love," Amelia said. "It finally came out under Acme. *That* was a disaster. No tension in that one at all. That's what it all depends on, tension." She looked around at the wrens. *"Sexual* tension."

The wrens tittered.

"But that wasn't why Julie wouldn't handle the book," Amelia said. "Julie was no fool. *She* knew Lydia for what she was. *She* wouldn't have let this travesty go on."

The wrens nodded in unison.

"It's too bad it wasn't this Lydia who died," Nick whispered in my ear. He was having trouble looking comfortable in a straight-backed, armless, fake Louis XVI chair. "We'd know right where to find the murderer."

"This is nothing," I whispered back. "She hasn't even started."

But Amelia had not only started, she had finished. She waved her teacup in the air, dismissing Lydia.

"Mary Allard," she said to me, changing the subject. "I suppose you've heard she wants to sit on the Line Committee?"

"She's perfectly eligible," I said. "Her line isn't up for an award. No other line from her company is up for an award. And if that's what Julie wanted—"

"I don't believe Julie wanted it," Amelia said. "That letter has to be forged."

"Maybe," I said. "But I'm not so sure I want to be on the Line Committee. I haven't done the reading. I write for Fires of Love and two other lines at Farret. If Fires of Love won the award and I was on the committee, I'd *expect* people to protest."

"But Fires of Love won't win the award," Amelia said. "It's not possible."

"Not possible?" Phoebe looked a little pale, even under all that makeup.

"Of course not," Amelia said. "Fires of Love is a terrible line. Everybody knows that."

"I think 'everybody' is a bit much," I said gently. "I hear they're going to gross a hundred million this year. A lot of people think Fires of Love is a wonderful line."

"Oh," Amelia said. "The money." She fussed with her breastplate. "Of course, you have to listen to the money," she went on, "because that's what tells you what your readers want. I suppose it's not all that surprising that Fires was an initial success. But it can't last, dear Patience. The whole thing's ridiculous."

"What's ridiculous?" I asked. "I'm on my third Fires of Love book. It's got everything."

"Of course it does," Amelia said. "But it doesn't have anything *new*. There isn't one thing to distinguish that line from a dozen others, and there are dozens of others. Even that Allard woman's Passion Line has something—a quality to it, a distinctive style. Fires of Love is just old-fashioned formula romance of the worst kind."

Phoebe laughed. "It certainly has a formula," she said. "A nine-page tip sheet."

"Every line has a tip sheet," I argued. "For God's sake, Phoebe. If they didn't have tip sheets, I couldn't write them."

"I suppose you don't have enough romance in your life," Amelia sighed. "That's true of so many young people these days. No romance. No passion. I don't know what you live for." She gave Nick a leer that made him jump in his chair. Then she got heavily to her feet. "I've got to go down the hall for a minute," she said. "I'll be right back."

She lumbered carefully away, swaying from side to side like a crippled ship. Phoebe and Nick and I sat still in our chairs, listening, waiting. This seemed like the perfect chance, but we had to be sure. We didn't want to be waylaid by the wrens, or overheard. Then we heard the sound of running water and the barely perceptible tinkle of glass.

"She's got a utility room," Phoebe said.

"Like a dressing room," I said. "With a sink."

"Plus a refrigerator," Nick said. "One of those."

"Maybe I ought to see if she needs help," I said, getting up. "Maybe she needs help carrying things."

"Oh no," one of the wrens said, while her sisters looked horrified. "Oh, no, Miss McKenna, *please*. It really isn't necessary. Guests don't need to do a thing around Miss Samson, not a thing. Maybe I'll just go check on her—"

"No, no," I said, backing quickly toward the nearest door. "It's not any trouble, really. I'll just go along here," I opened a set of double doors in Chinese lacquer red and slipped through to the other side, "and I won't be a minute."

The double doors gave onto a small, darkened sitting room, which gave onto a narrow hall, at the end of which was a dim, shadowy light. I could hear the sound of water running and the heavy thud of something hard hitting against tile. I tiptoed into the hallway and looked down the passage to Amelia, standing in the open door of the utility room, pouring something into a small, clear plastic cup.

"Amelia?" I called softly, edging down the hall.

She whirled around and squinted at me. "What is it?" she demanded. "Can't I even attend to myself in peace?"

"I'm sorry to bother you like this," I said, squeezing past her into the white-tiled, square little room. The overhead light was bright white and harsh, making Amelia's skin, even under the thick coat of foundation and cherry-red rouge, look dead. I leaned against a narrow strip of wall beside the half-sized refrigerator. "I didn't want to talk in front of the —the ladies." I had been about to call them "wrens."

Amelia took a sip from her plastic glass and gave me the fisheye. She didn't say anything. I didn't know where to start. What if she had never seen the envelope? What if she pretended she hadn't? I couldn't begin to imagine myself describing those pictures to her. No Amelia Samson novel had ever featured an unvirginal heroine—or allowed two people to make their way to bed without benefit of a wedding reception for at least a thousand guests. In the world of *Love's Finest Flower*, there was no crime, or death, or perversion. There was certainly no blackmail.

I cleared my throat and said, "It's about an envelope. Julie—"

I felt my back hit the wall before I even knew I had moved. My head knocked against the crack between the wall and the refrigerator. My arms shot out at both sides and hit the sharp edges between the tiles.

"Where is it?" Amelia hissed, shaking me hard. "Who gave it to you? What have you done with it?"

"Amelia, put me *down.*"

Instead, she lifted me again and gave me another shake.

"I mean to have it back," she said. "You won't get anything out of me. I won't pay you."

"Amelia," I choked out, "for God's sake, put me down. I don't want you to pay me anything. I just have this thing and I don't know what to do with it."

She gave me the fisheye again, but she let me go. She turned around and brought out the plastic glass and the gin bottle and poured the first full of the second. It was then I noticed the cigarette lying lit in the ashtray behind her, its smoke nearly invisible in the glare of the overhead light.

She made a little smile. "So you didn't know I drank," she said. "And you didn't know I smoked cigarettes. And there were a few other things you didn't know I did."

"Amelia, I didn't go looking for the damn thing," I said. "Someone just gave it to me."

"Who?"

"A fan," I said, blushing slightly. "Some fan gave Julie a manuscript, and Julie meant to give the fan one of those information packets, and instead she gave the fan the envelope. Anyway, the fan—"

"Don't lie to me," Amelia said. "Julie Simms never had that envelope. Julie Simms never saw it. Julie Simms never even knew it existed. The only people who knew were Myrra and myself."

"What about the person who gave it to you?"

"Never mind who gave it to me," Amelia said. "I want to know where you got it."

I took a deep breath. "I'm sorry," I said. "I'm sorry, Amelia, but that's really what happened. Two women came up to me in the lobby—"

"You're sorry." She sat down on a low stool, her monstrous legs pushing against the fabric of her dress, her cigarette between thumb and forefinger, the smoke drifting into my eyes. "Do you know how much I'm worth?"

"No," I said. "No, I don't."

"Neither do I. But it's a lot of money, Miss Patience Campbell McKenna, Miss White Anglo-Saxon Protestant Foxcroft School to Greyson College Junior Assemblies *bitch.* "

"It was Emma Willard," I said automatically.

"Do you realize I never have to write another word again, as long as I live? I've got enough money to buy the state of Connecticut and recharter it as my own private monarchy, if I want to. You all think you're so bloody wonderful. You and Phoebe Jewess Weiss. You and Julie Beauty Queen Simms. You and that little priss-faced Williams woman. Do you know where we came from, Myrra and me?"

"Amelia—"

"Let me tell you," she said, draining her glass again and pouring yet another. "Let me tell you, Miss Women's Liberation Was All My Idea. Where I came from it was the boys who went to college. I quit school at fourteen and went to work in the steam room of a laundry, because we needed the money to send my brother to the goddamn university. The University of Nebraska. A cow college. Cheap, right? Except it was the middle of the Depression and my father's store went bankrupt and then the job he got laid him off, but we were going to eat beans for ten years to be sure my brother went to college. My family was like that. Most families were, then. It didn't matter if the girls got an education, because the girls were getting married.

"Well, I got married. I was sixteen and I'd had the sweat coming down my back for two years and I'd had it. You know what that's like? You're always hot and you're always wet and the water gets in your clothes and the dye runs until you're the color of whatever you've been wearing, blue and green and yellow from those cheap dyes sinking into your skin. So I got married.

"I had a wonderful wedding in a church, because that's something else families paid for, big weddings for the daughters. I stood up there in a white veil and said 'I do' to the handsomest man I ever met and the most charming, and it was two years and two babies later I realized it wasn't the Depression, the bastard couldn't get a job, didn't want a job, and wouldn't hold it if it was forced on him. So I gave the two babies to my mother and I went back to the goddamn laundry, and then two things happened."

The squint she gave me was like the evil eye. "Two things happened," she repeated. "First, my brother ran away to the war and got himself killed in a training camp exercise, end of the Bright Young Man who was going to Lift Us All From Poverty. Then I came home one night with my arms all mottled green and my money in my stocking and I decided I wasn't going to do it, I wasn't going to give it to that little whiskey hauler with his fine eyes and the brains of a pickled herring. I wasn't going to give it to him to go down to some bar and drink it all away, not that time. So I didn't. So he gave me a black eye."

She threw back her head and laughed, full and deep and bittersweet.

"Do you know what my mother said to me?" she asked. "Said it was my duty. Said God gave women their men to preserve and protect and bring to salvation, forever and ever, till death do ye part. Good old midwestern snake-oil-salesman fundamentalist, that was my mother. But that wasn't me."

She got off the stool and steadied herself against the sink.

"I'm going back to my tea," she said. "And to the best suite in this hotel and the best china and my own goddamn life. And if you think I'm going to pay you a red cent for what's in that envelope, you're out of your bloody mind. Put those pictures up on a bulletin in the lobby. I don't give a flying shit."

CHAPTER 16

I was out of there so fast, even Phoebe didn't see me go. I needed air. I hit the street just as it started to snow and headed west against the holiday crowds. It was late afternoon, the beginning of dusk, and street-lamps glowed faintly in halos of mist. This was the season I liked best in Manhattan: the crush along the major avenues, the snow-glitter and winking lights in the windows of the stores, the band of angels in Rockefeller Center. I was passing a choir in full uniform singing *Adeste Fidelis* on the steps of Saint Patrick's Cathedral when I realized I might not get home to my niece and nephews in Connecticut this year. I might not wake up too early Christmas morning to paw through a Christmas stocking limp with age and drooling Hershey's kisses through its heel. I might very well be in jail.

Amelia and Myrra, I thought, wondering if a thirty-year-old woman who still looked forward to her mother's Christmas stocking was entirely sane. I couldn't seem to concentrate on anything. Images floated in and out: Julie and Myrra, Camille, Nick Carras, a friend of mine at college who had committed suicide by hanging herself from the over-head heating pipe in her room. I turned onto Sixth Avenue thinking it all came together somehow, and I was well into Times Square before I realized I wasn't making sense.

It couldn't have been after five o'clock, but it was dark. Times Square in the early darkness is full of noise and people, exciting the way a roller coaster is exciting, dangerous yet safe. I walked close against the walls of buildings, looking at posters for Broadway shows and X-rated movies, trying to see past the blinking neon lights and oil-grimed windows to the inner room of a storefront theater called only "Live! Girls! Live!" and promising "Ladies Night Thursday—Ladies Admitted

Free." Covering the narrow doorway was a larger-than-life-size, fully lit, plastic Santa Claus, a string of blue and yellow lights spelling out "Noel" beneath him.

On impulse, I left the main thoroughfare and went down a side street lined with stores only a few feet wide, each selling buttons, or badges, or erotic underwear for men—it didn't matter, as long as the item was highly specific and physically small, so that dozens and dozens of examples could be displayed against black velveteen in the window. On this street, the men who sat in the doorways looked tired and old and drunk, and the women paced back and forth in half a dozen sweaters, talking to themselves. I walked to the far end of the block and stopped in the coffee shop to order a hot chocolate to go, milk added. From the window, I could see the darkness leading to the river and feel the first cold of real menace, the promise of the kind of death Myrra had had. Something was moving out there, I could see it, although I couldn't distinguish it from the pattern of shadows made by dimming streetlamps and the fitful echo of Broadway's neon glare.

I took my hot chocolate, determined to get back to the Square and take the first cab I could find. Someone had told me once that there were roving packs of dogs near the river, worse than wolves, human-hating. I stepped out into the dark and told myself the river was a long way away, blocks and blocks, and I wasn't obliged to go down that street looking for something I didn't want to find. I couldn't shake the feeling I'd already found it. The drunks in the doorway had turned to ooze and regenerated into the octopus nightmares of my childhood, sliding and growing, soundless, under my feet.

I crossed the street and made myself stop, almost exactly in the middle of the block, at the window of a store selling "love aids." I drank hot chocolate and stared at the barb-tipped leather bullwhips, nail-studded leather face masks, a pair of leather panties with a dildo strapped to the front, its sides bristling with fine metal wires. The machinery of sadomasochism—a joke in college dormitories everywhere on those nights everyone stays up too late, dressed in nightgowns and robes, drinking gin and grenadine from coffee mugs.

The sound of feet in high-heeled leather shoes, walking too slowly, staying too far behind.

I turned toward the light spilling out from the Square and started walking, weaving in and out of the old women with their sweaters and their songs. Half a block, a short block, a street and not an avenue, and whatever was coming up behind me was young and female, a hooker, nothing to worry about, no one I knew.

I turned the corner on Ninth Avenue and stopped, breathless, in the light from a record store. It was fully dark and bitterly cold, making my lips and knuckles feel dry and chapped. I read every word on the cover of an album by Kim Carnes, and then I heard them again.

The sound of a woman in high-heeled leather shoes, walking slowly, walking raggedly, catching up.

I turned downtown, toward the light, and tried to pick up speed. Every few feet another man in another cap pushed another piece of paper into my hands. It was impossible to refuse them, and I found myself filling my pockets with cardboard cards in cheap pastels and slick, shiny brochures full of women exercising with weights. Pregnancy tests and health spas, free film and menswear sales, it didn't matter. There was no time to stop and no time to notice, until I was suddenly below Forty-second Street, on a part of Ninth Avenue as bleak and deserted on a Saturday as a warehouse district, but filled instead with iron-shuttered stores and the sound of those shoes.

I stepped over a drunk and moved into the shelter of a doorway to wait, conscious that I was doing the wrong thing. I should have been heading for the street, moving out into traffic, waving for a taxi or a cop. Instead, I leaned into my doorway, feeling small, tiny, infinitesimal, and nearly hysterical.

I closed my eyes and listened to the shoes, coming closer, coming faster, the sharp edge of the heel hitting the pavement like the sound of a fork against an empty glass. I waited until the very last moment. I waited until I could hear her breathing, coming painful and short against the cold. Then I stuck out my arm and grabbed the sleeve of her coat.

And stared right into the face of Lydia Wentward as she screamed.

CHAPTER 17

"That's what I need," Lydia cooed at me. "They won't mind. Nobody minds. Nobody sees. Just what I need."

She put the edge of the small, silver tube against the fine white line of cocaine she had strung out along the dark wood restaurant table and sucked it up, using first one nostril and then the other. It went so fast I hardly noticed it.

"Sterling silver," she told me, waving the tube in the air. "Got a sterling silver case, too. Bought them in a fancy jewelry store in Philadelphia. Nobody minds. They put needles in their arms in the bathrooms here."

"Not the same," I said, not doubting the story about the bathrooms. "If he sees you, he has to call the police."

"He won't call the police. He wouldn't call the police if I stabbed someone at the bar." She blinked at me and giggled. "Stabbing, stabbing," she said. "That's all we think about these days. Stabbing."

"Right," I said. I saw the waiter and signaled, wanting to get something heavily alcoholic into me before trying to find out what Lydia had been doing in Times Square, why she had been following me, why she hadn't called out to get my attention. Then I reminded myself that she might not have been following me at all, that it might have been a coincidence, but I couldn't swallow it. I couldn't stomach this bar either, a lightless cave of cheap liquor and watered drinks just off the Forty-second Street meat strip.

The waiter came to the table, his fists in the pockets of his dirty white apron, his eyes on Lydia's, smirking.

"Johnnie Walker Red on the rocks," I said, hoping to forestall the almost inevitable Jack Daniel's green label. "And she'll have a bottle of Heineken beer."

"No Heineken," he said. "Budweiser, Miller, Molson's."

"Molson's," I said.

"Molson's." He gave us an exaggerated bow and left, swaying as he walked, in no particular hurry.

"Stabbing," Lydia said, "is what it's all about."

"Is that what you were going to do tonight? Stab me in Times Square?"

Her eyes seemed to get wider and wider until the lids collapsed, shut tight against a fit of giggles.

"I can't stab you. Not unless I buy one of those things the dykes wear, and I wouldn't do that anyway, that's second best. Third best. Men are second best and this is the best of all." She waved her purse in the air. "Do you know there are a hundred and four separate terms for screwing?"

"And you know every one of them."

"I'm keeping a list. In a notebook." She leaned across the table until I could smell the dry garlic on her breath. "You know where I was? I was at Chappie's."

"What's Chappie's?"

"*You* know. You were there. I saw you in the street."

"I was in the street getting hot chocolate. I wasn't at Chappie's."

She sat back and pouted. "*She* wouldn't let me go there. She said it was bad for me. But it isn't."

"Who wouldn't let you go there?"

"Julie. Julie said I was going to get arrested, or crazy, but that was stupid, because if I'm not crazy now, I won't be."

"Maybe you are crazy now," I said. "What were you doing following me? Why didn't you just yell out? I thought you were trying to kill me."

"They do that, too," she said, her eyes lighting up. "On the top floor. Nobody's supposed to know about it, but I do."

"What do they do?"

"Kill people and take movies of it," Lydia said placidly. "Girls."

I reached automatically for my cigarettes, not really believing her, not disbelieving her either. I didn't know what to think or how to react. I couldn't decide if she was stoned or crazy. I lit up and tossed the pack to her, because she seemed to want it, and then the waiter came with the drinks. The scotch was watery and the Molson's came with a filthy glass, but it was a welcome change.

"Four-fifty," the waiter said.

I came up with a five.

"Keep it," I said.

He gave us another exaggerated bow.

"Too fat," Lydia said as he walked away. "They're all too fat."

"Who are?"

"Johns," Lydia said. "That's what we used to call them. Maybe they still call them that. Long time ago." She sucked meditatively on her beer. "Did I show you what I got today? I got a real good one today. First class."

She rolled up her sleeve and waved her arm in my face, then laid it down on the table and held it still. I took a deep drag and stared at the welts, the puncture marks, the razor-thin *S* curves of dried blood.

"All over me," she said with satisfaction. "All over my—titties." She let out a screeching giggle, choking a little as the sulfur from her match went up her nose. She threw it still burning in the ashtray and lit another.

"Look at this," she said. She pulled up the hair at the back of her neck and showed me what looked like a cross between a scar and a tattoo, a small black outline of a heart with the letter *S* inside. "I got that in 1944, when I was eighteen years old. I'm fifty-five. Did you know that?"

"No," I said, thinking: *Phoebe. I'll call Phoebe.*

"I'm fifty-five. I'm the only old whore you'll ever know who didn't end up a bag lady. That's supposed to be a secret. *She* said they wouldn't publish my books anymore if they knew. But she's dead, isn't she?"

"Julie?" I said. "Yes, Julie's dead."

"She made me grow my hair. Even when they had those hairdos, back in the sixties, like Mia Farrow. She always made me wear it long. To cover up *this.*" She flipped her hair back over the scar. "I like *this.* I was eighteen when I got it. I was pretty."

"I'm sure you were." Phoebe wouldn't be there. Phoebe would be at a meeting and then at dinner.

"No, you're not," Lydia said. "I look like shit. I'm fifty-five and I look a hundred and six and I don't give a damn. I don't give a damn I was a whore, either. I don't mind."

She sucked the rest of her beer out of the bottle and stood it on its head on the table.

"You know what?" she said. "I wasn't ever really pretty. Not like the girls who write for the category lines. Nice little girls from nice little houses on Main Street, every last one of them looking for the perfect man and the perfect wrinkle cream."

"Janine," I said. "We'll call Janine."

Lydia made a face. "The woman in the gray flannel suit. Gregory Peck was better-looking."

"Gregory Peck isn't waiting back at the hotel to get you your dinner."

Lydia shrugged. "Someday I'm going to go out and buy a shirtwaist dress," she said. "Little flower print, little belt, Peter Pan collar. Look like all the rest of you."

"Order another beer," I said. "I'll be right back."

I left another five on the table and hurried toward the back, past the single, slightly open door that said "Rest Room" to a small space by the kitchen where I knew there would be a pay phone. It was there and working, the fretful hum of the dial tone coming strong and sure. I dug out a dime and dialed the Cathay-Pierce.

"Could you page Miss Janine Williams?" I asked, when somebody finally answered the phone. "Try 1406."

"One moment please."

"Pay? Pay McKenna?"

I looked up and saw Lydia weaving and bobbing toward me, her hair loose, her shoulders slack, her legs buckling. She put out an arm to steady herself against the wall, inching toward me as if she was swimming through molasses.

"Just wanted to make sure you hadn't gone," she said. "Wanted to make absolutely sure."

"I haven't gone."

"Couldn't have you leave," Lydia said. "Not now. Not a good time to leave."

She gave me a smile that showed every one of her teeth and most of her gums and passed out at my feet.

CHAPTER 18

I poured a glass of water over her face, managing to wake her long enough to get her to her feet, through the main room of the bar, out to Broadway and into a cab. Her hair was wet when we hit the street, and I thought the cold bite of the strong wind would shock her awake. I was wrong. I had hardly given instructions to the cabbie when she closed her eyes and fell asleep again, her makeup running into thick lines of red and black and brown, making her face look like a Girl Scout's plaster of paris topographical map. I lit a cigarette and stared out the window in search of a clock. We'd found that cab too easily. It had to be late.

He pulled up to the Fifty-eighth Street side entrance to the Cathay-Pierce, and I paid him, opened the door closest to the curb, got out the street side and came around. Lydia lay across the seat, leaden and large, one false eyelash drooping down her cheek and a smile like a curlicue across her lips. I started to pull her by the legs into the narrow snow-covered ridge at the edge of the sidewalk.

"For God's sake," someone said. "There you are. Where have you been?"

"What's the matter, lady?" the driver said. "You want me to sit around at the curb for the next six months? You want that, I'm going to put the meter back on."

I looked up into the face of Nick Carras, high-cheekboned and clear. I didn't stop to wonder what he was doing there.

"I need some help," I told him. "She's out, deadweight, incapacitated. You still interested in being my lawyer?"

"Why?"

"Because this comes under the heading of privileged information."

"Privileged communications." He leaned down and picked Lydia off the seat, holding her in his arms like a parody of the old Boys' Town poster. I gave a ten-second tribute to the way he looked in his jeans and slammed the cab door shut.

"Is there some way we could sneak her upstairs?" I asked. "A back elevator. If we could call her doctor—"

"She doesn't need a doctor. She's asleep." He held her out to me. "Listen. Even, regular breathing, reasonably deep."

"Also beer, cocaine, and God knows what else," I said. "As well as *Time, Newsweek,* and half the staff of the 'CBS Evening News.' If they see her like this, it'll be everywhere."

"Will it matter?"

"Romance readers tend to be little ladies in Iowa, Kansas, and Missouri. They do not take kindly to overdoses of white powders ingested in Forty-second Street bars."

"Okay," he said. He carried her to the revolving door, wedged them both into a single quarter, and waited inside until I came through. "I'll get her upstairs for you," he said, leading me through the deserted back hall behind the lobby, "but I don't think you're going to be able to keep it absolutely quiet. You're going to have to tell Martinez, anyway."

He stabbed the elevator button and looked as surprised as I felt when the door slid open. We stepped inside.

"Fourteen," I told him. "What does Martinez want?"

"That's why I've been looking for you," he said. "By order of one Phoebe Weiss, now Damereaux, I am supposed to find you, find out where you've been, and find a way to convince Martinez you're telling the truth." The door slid open on eight, revealing nothing. "Thank God," Nick said. "I figure we're all right unless somebody sees us."

The door opened on fourteen. I held it for him until he got Lydia out and down the hall. I followed, rummaging her handbag for keys. I found four prescription bottles of Quaaludes, one prescription bottle of phenobarbital, a tin of cocaine, a package of No Doz, half an ounce of marijuana, and a silver hip flask full of gin.

"Here we are," I said. I jiggled the hotel key in the lock and managed to swing the door open. "My God," I said, "what's she been doing in here?"

Nick stepped inside and blinked in confusion at the piles of underwear, papers, cigarette packages, romance novels, candy wrappers, and movie magazines that littered the floor.

"The maid comes in once a day," he said. "How can she do this in one day?"

"How am I supposed to know? Take her into the bedroom and I'll get Janine to get her doctor."

He put her down on the couch instead.

"You can't get Janine," he said. "She's downstairs talking to the police."

I stopped where I was and looked at him, feeling my stomach drop, feeling that numbness, which always covered me until the emergency was over, begin to fall away.

"Janine is talking to the police," I said. "Why?"

He sat down on the floor, his back against the couch where Lydia lay, and stretched out his legs. He looked more than ever like a Bennington freshman's concept of a Greek God. He sounded like the Voice of Death in an ancient morality play. Something was wrong and getting worse. I felt his growing pessimism as an accusation.

"I'm not exactly sure what's happening myself," he said. "After Phoebe and I finally escaped from Amelia, I went for a walk. I got back about half an hour ago. I walked through the door, the elevator opened on the other side of the lobby, and this guy ran out yelling somebody's dead. We all went running to the fifth floor. Phoebe came from another direction. She took one look at this woman and said I had to find you. Where were you, anyway?"

"Times Square." I motioned to Lydia on the couch. "I was taking a walk. I met Lydia and she was like that."

"Just like that?" He gave Lydia a once-over. "Just like that, on the street?"

"Of course not," I said. "Drunk or stoned or something. So I took her to a bar on Forty-second Street and bought her a beer. Where, as I told you, she decided to do just a little more cocaine."

"And passed out."

"Passed out or OD'd or went into a coma or worse." I gave Lydia a nervous look. "I think we ought to call the hospital. I don't know what she's swallowed or snorted I didn't see."

"You been with her for the last forty-five minutes?"

"For the last forty-five minutes I've probably been getting her in and out of cabs."

"What time did you leave the hotel?"

"You saw me leave the hotel," I said. "You saw me leave Amelia's, anyway. I went right out."

"Anybody see you leave?"

"I don't know," I said. "You and Phoebe. Amelia. What difference does it make?"

He closed his eyes and threw back his head, frowning slightly. "It could be totally unrelated," he said. "But I don't believe it."

He took a brown paper bag out of the pocket of his down vest and tossed it to me. "Baklava," he said. "Like this morning."

I took a largish piece from the bottom layer of wax paper.

"Let's get one thing clear," he said. "You did not, I take it, call Phoebe at six-fifteen this evening and ask her to meet you at six-thirty on the fifth floor of this hotel."

"Of course I didn't," I said. "I was—" I waved at Lydia, still inert on the couch.

"We knew somebody was probably setting you up," he sighed. "Why should today be any different? You go walking down Sixth Avenue, a nice leisurely stroll to clear your head. Wonderful idea. Can't prove any of it. While you're out hacking around, somebody calls Phoebe, claims to be you, and tells her she's *got* to be on the fifth floor at six-thirty. When she gets there, somebody has taken a knife to Leslie Ashe."

"Leslie Ashe?" I said. "Myrra's granddaughter Leslie Ashe?"

"She wasn't anybody I recognized," Nick said. "I wouldn't recognize her if she were this Leslie Ashe."

"*I* wouldn't recognize Leslie Ashe. I've never set eyes on the woman." I looked at Lydia, pale and dirty and tired. "I'd better call the doctor," I said. "And maybe I should get in touch with Phoebe. Find out—"

I stopped, feeling the pressure building up behind my eyes, the control draining out of my muscles.

"Leslie Ashe," I said. "For God's sake. What's *happening?*"

CHAPTER 19

Voices in a hallway, hysterical and ragged, sharp and querulous and high. Two officers in uniform, standing against a doorjamb, arms folded across chests.

"Warm water and soap, that'll get the blood out. Warm water and Ivory soap."

"Club soda by itself, before it sets."

"Can't take the glass up in the vacuum. Tear the bag to pieces."

"That's the Farret suite," I said, putting my hand on Nick's arm. The gesture slowed him enough to give me time to look over the scene: the crowd of young women in pastels huddled inches from the police line, Mary Allard with her hands and back pressed against the far wall, Janine in tears on the floor in a pile of papers. As we drew closer, I could see the blood, a thin stream emerging from the darkness of the suite, beginning to congeal.

Somebody grabbed my arm and swung me around.

"Where have you been?" Phoebe hissed at me. "Martinez will be here any minute. Have you seen Nick?" She saw Nick herself and nodded. "I've been going crazy, you've got no idea, and then I couldn't find you anywhere."

"What's wrong with Janine?" I asked her, pressing forward through the women. They were hard to move. Like the audience at an outdoor concert, they had chosen their positions and meant to keep them.

"Janine?" I called, a little louder than I had to and right into the ear of a fat girl with a string of fresh acne across her jaw. "Janine, are you all right?"

She rose off the floor, the papers streaming from her hands. They were sodden with blood.

I reached her and put my arm around her shoulder, thinking she must be hysterical. She looked down at the papers.

"It's seven o'clock," she said. "I need them for eight. I'll never get a new set in time, never." She wiped her eyes with the back of one hand. "I couldn't use these even if they weren't covered with blood," she told me. "They're evidence. Somebody tried to kill that girl and now they're evidence." She burst into another spate of tears.

I held her closer, letting her cheek brush my shoulder.

"There, there," I said. "It's all right."

"No, it isn't," Janine said. "We won't be able to compete. After all this work, and all the work to decorate the suite, and then this girl's dying . . . she must be dying, they won't let anyone in there, they're keeping it dark." She glared at the policemen.

"It's all right," I repeated, drawing her away from the door and into the crowd. She held furiously to her printout, the paper trailing behind us like what commercials like to call "bathroom tissue." I got her through the crowd to Phoebe.

"Janine thinks she's dead," I said.

"She's not even bleeding anymore," Phoebe said. "People are just being hysterical."

"Somebody stabbed her," Janine sniffled. "Over and over again. She was all cut up." She gulped loudly. "All over her face. And on her arm. There was so much *blood.*"

"There wasn't so much blood," Phoebe said. "There was a fair amount."

"Somebody called an ambulance," Janine said. "They never got here. And she isn't conscious. She's just *lying* there."

There was a sound of scraping metal and a bump. Somebody yelled "stand back" and we were pushed against the wall, flattened by the backward surge of the crowd. Two men in white uniforms came rushing out of the elevator, pushing what looked like a stretcher in front of them and making way for a small old man in a dirty gray suit with a doctor's bag in hand.

"Just a minute," I said. I had seen a break in the crush and I made for it, taking advantage of the confusion to get near the door. It was easier than I expected. Everyone's attention was concentrated on the ambulance men and the doctor, and even the two uniformed policemen were more occupied watching the medical procedure than controlling the crowd. I slipped behind one of them and through the door, holding my breath.

The room was dark, the overhead light a live wire circled by broken glass, the reading lamps overturned and shattered on the floor. Someone drew the curtains, letting in the pale glow of streetlamps, and in that light I could see the overturned chairs, the out-of-place end tables, the pile of books and papers on the floor. Someone had searched the room and done a very poor job of it.

"Spot," somebody said. The room lit up like the stage set of a talk show. I started backing toward the door, keeping my hands in my pockets. I didn't want my fingerprints in that place. That was all Martinez would need. It wouldn't take him long to find out I'd never been in that room before tonight.

I got out the door and into the crowd without being seen by the police and started to fight my way to Phoebe and Nick and Janine. The women had inched forward and compressed, each trying to get a look through that door. I stumbled against the fat, pimply girl and heard her say, "She fought for her life. Isn't that encouraging?"

I was going to ask the idiot what *else* she thought someone would do if they were being attacked by a maniac with a knife, but I didn't bother. I wasn't convinced she *had* fought for her life. The room didn't look like the scene of a struggle. There were no pieces of broken furniture, no torn curtains. The overhead light could not have been accidentally broken in a fight. It was nearly fourteen feet in the air.

I shoved against the fat girl one more time and made my way to the wall, expecting to find Phoebe waiting for me. Instead, I found a vacant corner, the paint peeling a little at the seam between the walls. Whatever view I might have had was blocked by the crowd moving backward again, pushed away from the door by one of the white-uniformed men.

"Stand back," someone bellowed up front. "Stand back. Clear a path. Stand back."

"Very polite crowd, aren't they?" someone said in my ear as a lane was duly cleared. "Always remember their manners."

I looked up at Mary Allard's little fox face, its promise of delicacy destroyed by the thick red slashes of rouge and lipstick.

I nodded toward the door. "Do you know what happened? Is she dead?"

"She's not dead." She turned her bright little eyes on the doorway, their malice mixed with something less definable. "I know what was *supposed* to happen," she said.

"I'd rather know what really happened," I said.

Mary shrugged. "That's the easy part," she said. "Miss Ashe walked into the Farret hospitality suite at six-thirty, when no one was there, and someone perfectly *terrible* came up behind her, and beat her up, and cut her up, and left the knife lying on the floor for anyone to see. Except, of course, Miss Ashe didn't come up at six-thirty. She came up at six." Mary bit her bottom lip with tiny, pointed teeth. "I came up with her in the elevator."

I looked at her suspiciously, but I didn't make the accusation she expected me to make.

"Maybe you just feel like causing a lot of trouble," I said. "That seems like what you're interested in lately."

"Am I?" she said, whirling around and grabbing my arm. "Am I really? The letter is genuine, you know. I can prove that. I *will* prove it."

"Let go of me."

"You're all going to try railroading me right out, and you probably will, but it won't be because that letter isn't genuine. It's genuine. In Julie Simms's own handwriting. And I'm not going to put up with this nonsense much longer. I'm not going to go on being avoided in dining rooms and snubbed at lunches and ignored at meetings."

"You're being paranoid."

She dropped my arm. "I'm tired to death of sucking up to the lot of you, smiling like a little dog, acting like I give a shit. I don't give a shit. And I'm definitely not going to let that little bitch get away with it."

"Who? Leslie Ashe? What did she do to you?"

"You know perfectly well I don't mean Leslie Ashe."

She gave me a last long look, then turned on her four-inch spikes and walked away.

I leaned back against the wall and closed my eyes. There was still noise in the corridor, Phoebe and Janine and Nick were lost in the crowd, someone might be dying. I didn't have the energy to cope with any of it.

Someone stepped on my foot and I wrenched away, my eyes opening automatically. The ambulance men were coming through the corridor with the stretcher, holding it the way firemen might once have held buckets in a water brigade.

The fat girl with the pimples shoved her elbow in my ribs. I shoved back, making her fall against the woman beside her. The movement put me in front of the crowd. I looked down, expecting to see nothing but a stretcher and a sheet made lumpy by the body beneath.

I saw the black hair, the pale, over-made-up face, the odd angle of neck on shoulders. I saw the rough dry streaks of clotting blood, the rhythmic rise and fall of the chest.

I saw Gamble Daere.

CHAPTER 20

I was supposed to go to the Line Committee meeting, but I didn't. I gave Phoebe a note withdrawing my candidacy, shook off Nick, and went back to the suite. I needed peace and quiet and a warm bath. I needed a chance to think about the fact that the times didn't match. They didn't match at all.

Someone had called Phoebe at six-fifteen, claimed to be me, and asked her to be on the fifth floor at six-thirty. Leslie Ashe had gone to the fifth floor at six. If someone was setting me up for the stabbing of Leslie Ashe, she had to *know* the woman would be there. Did she? Or was I supposed to be set up for something else? And what was Leslie Ashe doing in the Farret hospitality suite at six-thirty on a Saturday evening? The hospitality suites weren't to open to the public until Monday afternoon.

I threw half Phoebe's box of Wessingham's Old Lavender Bath Salts into the bottom of the tub and turned the water on full. Camille sat on the edge of the tub and contemplated the bubbles. She was both terrified and dauntless, and I liked the combination. I liked even more what she reminded me of: my parents' house at Christmas, snow on the front lawn and animals in the kitchen, my brother's children hiding in the secret passage at the side of the living room fireplace. News of Julie's murder had been on the six o'clock news. They must have seen it. I wondered what they thought of it.

Camille started to totter toward the water. I picked her up and sat down with my back against the wall, holding her in my arms. The bath carpet was stiffly, pleasantly irritating against my legs. My arms and shoulders ached.

I should call my brother George, I thought, letting my head fall back and my eyes close. My mother frightened me and my father, who had devoted himself for many years to the playing of bad tennis, wouldn't be much help. George and I understood each other. He was three years younger than I was, and he had always wanted to specialize in eleventh-hour rescues.

If I hadn't wanted to attend Myrra's funeral, I would have been in Connecticut when Julie died. I had intended being in Connecticut. I wanted to be there now. My mother might frighten me and my father be more charming than practical, but that big white house locked away by hedges made Eden a second-rate paradise.

Camille stretched out along my legs, curled up, prepared to sleep. I wondered why Myrra's earring had been in Julie's handbag and why she had had the blackmail envelope and why she was dead. I told myself I should turn off the water before it overflowed. I asked myself if Nick was single or going with someone of whom Phoebe did not approve. My back ached.

The phone woke me up. I opened my eyes to see the first thin lip of water edging over the rim of the tub. I dumped the cat on the floor and got up to turn off the tap. The phone was still ringing. I was going to have to answer it.

I took my robe from the back of the bathroom door and put Camille in the pocket of it. She stretched and settled and swung against me as I crossed the living room. I wanted the phone to stop, but it went on and on, hurting my ears.

I said hello, expecting Phoebe, or Nick, or even Mary Allard. I got Marian Pinckney instead.

Marian Pinckney was the definitive end to peace and quiet. Her voice ran through the night like a caterpillar in jogging shoes.

"Sorry," she said. "Early. Frantic. Couldn't wait."

I settled on the floor with my back against the couch. I had been so primed to resent this call, it was hard to find any pleasure in it. I reminded myself of how important it was. Marian Pinckney might have information I needed. I should be happy she had had the courtesy to call early.

"I shouldn't even be calling you about this," Marian said. "It's illegal for me to be calling you about this. I thought of calling you from a phone booth, but it would take too long."

"I'm sure nobody's tapping your phone," I soothed.

There was a rustling of papers. "Okay. Now. About the Samson account. It was opened the second of April, theoretically by Miss Samson herself, with one hundred dollars in cash. Since then there have been deposits of one thousand dollars a month on the first business day of every month and withdrawals—"

"Wait a minute," I said. "What do you mean *theoretically* opened by Amelia herself? Don't you guys ask for identification?"

Marian sighed. "Of course we ask for identification. Do you know how easy it is to get identification? Go read any paperback spy thriller. Millions of ways. Perfectly simple. The government will even help you with it. Besides, this is our regular checking account. It doesn't pay interest. No big problem. What I found in the file was an American Express number, which means no picture. We can't demand a driver's license or a passport, because a lot of people don't have them. And I don't think anybody bothered to check out the Amex."

"Most people don't hand out their American Express cards to black-mailers," I said.

"Whatever," Marian said. "The reason I got so excited was that we have another account, one we've had a little trouble with, and the record on that was one thousand dollars cash deposited the first business day of each month at a teller window. The same one thousand dollars was withdrawn in three installments of three hundred fifty, three hundred fifty, and three hundred dollars each at the twenty-four-hour instant teller at the branch on West Eighty-second Street on each of three succeeding Mondays following the deposit, except for this month. Got that?"

"I think so," I said. "Somebody goes to a teller and deposits a thousand in cash. Then someone goes to one of those computer terminals and uses it to withdraw the money in three installments. Why three installments?"

"Three fifty is the maximum you can get from the terminal in one day."

"Okay."

"Okay. Now. Here's what's wrong. First, there should have been a withdrawal from this account Monday, and there wasn't. Thursday morning, someone tried to use the card but punched the wrong code number, did it twice, and the computer ate it. This showed up on my desk Friday morning as part of a security report. I never read security reports. It's just that this was right on top of my desk, and it was the beginning of the alphabet, and—"

"Myrra Agenworth," I said. My stomach was beginning to claw at me.

"How did you know it was Myrra Agenworth?" Marian sounded suspicious. She should have been.

"Jesus Christ," I said. It was all I could think of.

"Jesus Christ *nothing,*" Marian said. "You want to swear? Listen to this. The address for the Agenworth account is a post office box in FDR station. The address for the Samson account is the *same* post office box in FDR station. I ran the address through the computer. Global search. Do you know what I found?"

"No."

"I found seven—count them, *seven*—active accounts with that mailing address. All opened with a hundred dollars cash. All using the same credit card for identification. All with the same pattern as the Agenworth account, one thousand in, three fifty, three fifty, three hundred out. All with deposits made on the first of this month and no withdrawals made since. All set up the first business day of April."

"I don't understand," I said. "Are you telling me someone made each of these people walk into a branch of the New York Guaranty Trust, open a checking account, keep it supplied with money, and then give out copies of their terminal cards and secret numbers?"

"No, no," Marian said. "I think your blackmailer did it all *himself.* Everything is withdrawn from West Eighty-second, but the accounts were opened all over the city, a different branch each time, and the deposits were made all over the place, too. The blackmailer goes to a branch, opens a checking account in his victim's name, then gets the paraphernalia mailed to the post office box. Then—"

"Then all she has to do is send copies of the incriminating information and a set of predated, preencoded slips to the victim, and the victim doesn't know who she's being blackmailed *by.*"

"Can't get caught, either," Marian said. "If he uses a phony credit card, or a stolen one, there's nothing to connect the blackmailer to the accounts."

"I think I'm going to have a headache."

"Get a pen," Marian said. "I'll give you the names on the accounts. If you find out anything—"

"I'll tell you," I promised.

"Okay," Marian said. "First—Agenworth, Myrra. Second—Wentward, Lydia. Third—Simms, Julie. Fourth—Williams, Janine. Fifth—Samson, Amelia. Sixth—Caine, Martin. Seventh—Damereaux, Phoebe Weiss." There was a pause. "You know any of these people?"

"All of them," I said. "I know all of them." Phoebe's name was floating in the air like Casper, the Friendly Ghost. Phoebe was my best friend. Why wouldn't she tell me if she was being blackmailed?

"Pay?" Marian Pinckney said. "This Phoebe parenthesis Weiss unparenthesis, is she Phoebe Weiss from Greyson?"

"Yes," I said. What had Phoebe done? What could she possibly do?

"Little Phoebe Weiss with all the bags of food in her room? All the kosher stuff? She's that crazy writer with the diamonds?"

"Yes," I said, not really listening. "Yes, she is."

"Well, hot damn," Marian said. "I'll have to go out and get some of her books. God knows they're all over the place. Tell her if she needs a personal banker, tax help, investment advice, that kind of thing, tell her to call me."

"I will."

"Good. Fine. Tremendous. Now I have to get back and straighten this thing out. Or at least figure out how to tell the president about it without getting canned."

She hung up in my ear. I hardly noticed. All I could think of was: what in the name of God had Phoebe *done?*

CHAPTER 21

When Phoebe got back to the suite, I was still in the unreconstructed Victorian bathroom, rescuing Camille from her flying leap into the claw-footed bathtub. She had been trying to catch bubble bath. I got her before she sank for the last time, dunked her once more to get off the soap, and dried her on a thick gold bath towel with *CP* inscribed in blue embroidery beneath a red embroidered crown. Then I put on a terry cloth robe and put her in the pocket.

In the living room, Phoebe was sitting on the couch, unwinding strand after strand of rope diamonds and looking tired. For once it wasn't badly applied eyeliner or myopically decorative rouge. It was quarter after eleven, and she looked as wasted as she would after an all-night martini binge.

"How was the meeting?" I asked her, coming to sit beside her on the couch.

She shrugged. "I didn't stay for the end of it. They're going to take Mary, though why you did what you did, I don't know. Janine's about ready to kill you."

"I forgot she was so dead set against Mary." That was true. The last thing I'd been thinking of when I wrote my note was what Janine thought about the makeup of the Line Committee. It was the last thing I was thinking of now.

"Oh, well," Phoebe was saying. "You know Janine. As far as she's concerned, *once* someone's done something wrong, you can never trust them again. It's a good thing she never had children."

"She still could," I said. "She's only forty-two or -three. And besides." I took a deep breath. "She must have done something once, something someone could blackmail her for."

Phoebe looked at me curiously. "Marian called," she said. "I was so busy down there, I forgot all about it. What did she say?"

I explained the blackmail scheme as it had been explained to me. She was brighter about it than I had been. She nodded all the way through my recital, and then said, "So the only time anyone ever saw the blackmailer was when she opened the account, and then only the bank officer. Nobody who could recognize her. So nobody knows who she is."

"Right," I said. It was hard not to stare at her. How could she sit there and not tell me anything? How could she go on pretending it had never happened?

She was shaking her head. "I've got the same objections you had this morning," she said. "Myrra would never let herself be blackmailed. And Amelia said she'd never pay it."

"Except that Amelia *must* have paid it," I said. "Deposits were being made to her account as late as the beginning of this month, right before Julie's murder. And into Julie's."

Phoebe sank into the couch, the action as much a response to surprise as to tiredness.

"Julie? What could Julie have done that someone could blackmail her for?"

"A week ago, I wouldn't have said any of them could have done anything somebody could blackmail them for. Then we find out Myrra and Amelia were lovers. Lydia used to be a hooker. That's three out of the seven. God only knows what the rest of them have done."

"Well, the idea of Janine is ridiculous," Phoebe said. "She's the original old maid. She doesn't even *drink.*"

"She's been paying blackmail for nine months," I said, "and a lot of it. A thousand dollars a month is a lot of money."

"It's impossible," Phoebe insisted. "Do you know what a romance editor makes? Twenty to twenty-five, tops. Where's Janine getting it?"

"I don't know," I said. "But she's paying it. One thousand dollars a month cash every month since April."

"No way," Phoebe said, shaking her head back and forth and muttering into the velvet of her caftan. "No physical way. She'd have to sell cocaine on the side just to make the payments, and it's not like she's starving to death. She's got nice clothes. She goes out to dinner. She's got a beautiful apartment. She has a subscription to the Metropolitan Opera."

I got off the couch and began pacing the carpet, letting Camille ride on my shoulder where she could feel superior. I was so tired, colors and shapes had begun to blend into each other.

"What you're saying is that Marian has to be wrong about Janine," I said. "Janine is not being blackmailed."

"Maybe it's a different Janine Williams," Phoebe said.

"Maybe it's a different Phoebe Damereaux."

She shot me a look, suddenly alert, suddenly wary.

"What do you mean?" she demanded. "Nobody's ever tried to blackmail me."

"Fine," I said. "Tell me there are two Phoebe (Weiss) Damereaux's."

"But that's *ridiculous,*" Phoebe exploded. She jumped off the couch and began pacing beside me, throwing her hands in the air and shouting. "I haven't done anything anyone could blackmail me for. And you should know. Goddammit, you know my whole life story. We've been living in each other's laps for the past nine years. What have I ever done? Just name one thing I've ever done I could be blackmailed for."

"How am I supposed to know what you've done?" I shouted. "How am I supposed to know what you did five years ago you're not so happy about now? Maybe you took a black lover and don't want your parents to know. Maybe you took a Jewish lover but he didn't want to marry you and you had an abortion, which you also wouldn't want your parents to know. Maybe you took an *Arab* lover—"

"I can't be blackmailed about any lovers," Phoebe shouted. "I haven't had any lovers. I'm a virgin, you asshole!"

The word "virgin" stopped the conversation dead. We stared at each other, Phoebe in a state of blushing embarrassment and me in shock. Then I threw myself into the nearest chair and said, "Jesus, Phoebe. You can't be a virgin."

"Why not?"

"You just can't, that's all."

"Give me one good reason why not."

"All right," I said, coming near shouting again. *"The Catewall Inheritance,* pages 277 to 301."

"Oh," Phoebe said. *"That."* She walked with almost unreal dignity to the couch, sat down, and crossed her feet at the ankles and her hands in her lap. "I made it up."

"You made it up? Phoebe, there were things in those love scenes I'd never even *heard* of."

"I have a very good imagination."

"That's putting it mildly."

"And I did research," Phoebe said. "I went to bookstores and read through those manuals they have. There isn't one thing in that book you couldn't find out by going to Barnes and Noble."

I closed my eyes and sighed. "It wouldn't have occurred to me," I said. "And how did you end up thirty years old and a virgin? In *New York?"*

She started pacing again.

"I was too fat in college," she said. "And I'm too fat now, really, except it probably wouldn't matter except I have so much work to do. I mean, five years ago I made exactly four thousand dollars from my writing and I hardly met the rent, for God's sake."

"Also, you were chicken."

"Also, I was chicken," she agreed. "I'm still chicken."

"That's okay." I hauled myself out of my chair. "You couldn't be blackmailed for that? Because you're a virgin? You know, America's sexiest romance novelist—"

"Don't be ridiculous. If anybody said I was a virgin, I'd deny it. Nobody would believe it, anyway."

"True," I said. "They'd find it hard to swallow even if they knew you. But Phoebe, *somebody's* been putting a thousand a month into an account in your name for the past nine months."

"And in an account in Myrra's name," Phoebe said.

"Also Lydia, Janine, Julie, Amelia, and Marty Caine."

"Amelia's probably asleep," Phoebe said.

"Lydia's in no condition," I said.

"Janine and Marty were going to have a drink in the Castle Walk after the Line Committee meeting," Phoebe said innocently. "The meeting's probably not even over yet."

"Could go on to midnight," I said.

"Marty will be drinking all alone," Phoebe said.

I headed for the bedroom to find my socks.

CHAPTER 22

I had my pants half on when Barbara called. It was one of those conversations, misdirected and circuitous, that make me want to buy an answering machine.

"He *just* left," Barbara said. "I mean, I just got him out of here. I had to call the police."

"What was he doing?" Camille latched on to one of the buttons on my shirt and pulled mightily. I detached her, rescued a sock from under the night table, and sat down on the bed. Phoebe stood in the door, jumping up and down and pointing at the watch she didn't wear.

"This time he was leaving a note," Barbara said. "The note's sitting there, right on your door."

"You didn't look at it?"

"I wasn't going out there while he was lurking in the hall."

"Is he still lurking in the hall?"

"No."

"Then why don't you get it for me now? You can read it to me on the phone."

There was a pause.

"Just a minute," Barbara said finally.

I put the phone on the bed. With all those locks to open and secure, I was counting on a good five minutes before hearing about the note.

"Why," I asked Phoebe, "do I feel Nick is going to swoop in here and kill us?"

"Nick went back to his apartment," Phoebe said.

"He's going to be furious when he hears about this," I said. "He hates us doing anything on our own. I don't understand—"

I heard sounds on the other end of the line and lifted the receiver to my ear.

"Hello?" Barbara said. "Pay? Are you still there?"

"I'm still here."

"It's not a note, exactly." There was a sound of rustling paper. "It's a telephone number." She read it off.

I said, "just a minute" and got up to rummage in my tote bag for pen and paper. I came up with a Saks bill and a Bic that had obviously been leaking over everything for months.

"Give it to me again," I told Barbara. She repeated it.

"Do you know what exchange that is?" I asked her. "I don't think it's the West Side."

"I thought you'd recognize it," she said. "He left it on your door. Without a note." She took a deep breath. "I don't think it's fair to have him wandering around the halls like that. Lurching. He's always lurching."

"I thought you said he was lurking."

"Both. And he has to be someone you know, Pay. Someone you didn't know wouldn't come sneaking around the apartment, dead drunk, two days in a row, and then leave a phone number."

"You're sure it wasn't Daniel?"

"Of course I'm sure it wasn't Daniel. I've never seen this man before."

"Well, he probably isn't anyone I know," I said. "Just a nut. He read about the murder in the papers and wants to annoy me. I'd give the note to Martinez if I were you."

"I will. Can I watch *Mary, Queen of Scots* at your place tomorrow night?"

"Are the police seals off?"

"They will be."

"Go ahead then."

"Thanks a lot."

She hung up without saying good-bye. I hung up, too, looking down at the number in my hand. Just a nut, I told myself. Just some drunk off the street with a nasty mind and no sense of other people's privacy. I didn't have to dial the number if I didn't want to.

I didn't have to go back to West Eighty-second Street, either. I thought of Barbara sitting on my couch, watching in the dark while Mary Stuart stretched her neck over a stone and waited for the axe. Was there still blood on my carpet? Still a chalk mark on the floor? When this was over, I was going to find a new apartment and move in clean. My old landlord could have my typewriter and my wicker chair and my two Calvin Klein skirts—and the smell of blood and urine that went with them.

I found my shoes and pulled them on. Marty and Janine, I reminded myself. We were supposed to be concentrating on Marty and Janine.

We found Marty alone at a window table in the Castle Walk, his shoes off, his legs stretched across a vacant chair, his fifth straight scotch a thin amber puddle at the bottom of his glass. Phoebe looked at the scotch and made second-thoughts noises, but I pushed her on. I had to push her on. Things were making less sense by the minute. For the moment, Marty was our only chance to find the key.

He saw the waitress and us at the same time. He said something to the waitress, then waved us over.

"That meeting finally over?" he said. "The bitch goddess is supposed to be joining me for a drink, but no show." He grinned lewdly at Phoebe. "You want to marry me?" he asked her.

Phoebe cleared her throat. I scraped my chair against the carpet. I had no idea how to start this conversation. Was I supposed to just ask him if he'd been paying blackmail for nine months? What kind of niceties led up to a question like that? I had never seen Marty drunk before, never heard him call Janine "bitch goddess." For all I knew, he secretly hated us all, and would be as little inclined to help as Martinez.

For all I knew, he was too drunk to remember his date of birth. The waitress brought three glasses of straight scotch. Marty paid for them.

"You two look looey," he said. "You should be celebrating. The frame didn't work this time. Leslie Ashe lives. Leslie Ashe lives and tells the world she was *not* attacked by Patience Campbell McKenna.'

"Where did you hear that?" I sat up very straight in my chair. "Did you talk to the police?"

"I talked to the bitch goddess," Marty said. "She got a call from the woman. Keep her place at the dinner tomorrow night, quote unquote. She's coming to the cocktail party. It was just a scratch. Something like that."

"It wasn't just a scratch," Phoebe said. "There was a lot of blood."

Marty shrugged. "I didn't see it," he said. "The bitch goddess saw it, but all she can talk about is her printouts. God, that woman is amazing. Marty do this. Marty do that. Marty, go back and run it again. Do you realize I actually did that? I even came here with the rerun in time for her idiotic presentation. Amazing."

He took a large swallow and finished half his drink, leering at Phoebe again. I took a sip of mine, had a few muscle spasms as it went down my throat, then felt my arms and shoulders go slack. I should have thought of it before, I decided. I should have locked myself in Phoebe's suite and stayed drunk for the weekend.

Phoebe poured half an inch of scotch into her very large glass of water and took a tentative sip. She made a face.

"This won't do," she said. Then she looked at Marty. "Are you too drunk to answer questions?"

He raised an eyebrow. "Answer questions about what?"

"About blackmail," Phoebe said. I nearly grabbed her under the table. She sat in her little-Miss-Prim-at-dancing-class pose, hands folded in her lap, ankles probably crossed and feet not quite touching the floor, and said, "We want to know if you've been paying a thousand dollars a month in blackmail to an account in the New York Guaranty Trust."

Marty's surprise lasted less than a minute. After that, he let out a whoop like a war yell. He couldn't contain himself.

"A thousand dollars a month," he said. "My God, I don't bring home a thousand a month. I don't have a thousand dollars in one place. I couldn't get it. I don't have that much credit on my VISA card."

"I didn't ask you that," Phoebe said. "I asked you if you were paying it in blackmail."

Marty blinked. "You're serious," he said. He sounded surprised that Phoebe could be serious about anything. He shook his head. "No," he said. "I have not been paying one thousand dollars a month into an account in the New York Guaranty Trust for blackmail. I haven't been paying blackmail, period."

He looked from one of us to the other, soberer now, speculative. "You two want to tell me what this is all about?"

I got ready to clap my hand over Phoebe's mouth, but I didn't need to. She had decided she'd given out enough information. She stirred her water and scotch and frowned at the table.

"I thought all you people made a lot of money," she said. "Marketing. Sales."

"Yeah," Marty said. "The sales guys make out all right with the commissions. With marketing it depends on who you are. I'm the trash flack." He laughed. "I also haven't been doing too well until recently. First Romantic Life. Then old F of L didn't pick up till the February returns, didn't really take off till March. I thought we were all going to get fired. Sometimes I still feel that way."

"With a hundred million in the first year?" I was skeptical.

Marty shrugged. "A hundred million and a lot of problems," he said. "I've got to give the bitch goddess one thing. She knows the problems. She even knows the solutions." He knocked reverently on the table. "May we win a little gold statuette," he said.

I decided not to tell him about Amelia's conviction that Fires of Love would *never* win a Brontë. I also decided it was time to leave. I was tired and the conversation was going nowhere. We could talk to Janine tomorrow.

Phoebe was so preoccupied, I had to pull her to her feet. She smiled and nodded at Marty with all the genuineness of a windup tin soldier. I pushed her out of the Castle Walk and into the lobby.

"Wake up," I hissed in her ear. "You can sleep when we get back to the suite."

The elevator doors opened. I pushed her inside and punched the button for our floor.

"What's the matter with you?" I demanded. "You're acting like you're on dope."

"It's Fires of Love," Phoebe said. "It has to be." Suddenly she didn't look dreamy at all, but small, and sick, and very upset. "There's something wrong at Fires of Love," she repeated.

"How do you know?"

"That list. Of the blackmail accounts." She giggled like a drunk with the hiccoughs. "It's the Fires of Love Advisory Board and the Fires of Love Marketing Director and the Fires of Love Editor in Chief."

The elevator doors slid shut.

"It was my idea, you know," Phoebe said. "The Advisory Board was. I suggested it to Janine."

In the dark, the Primrose Suite of the Cathay-Pierce could have been our old dorm room at Greyson. Ordinarily, only freshman share rooms at Greyson. Upperclassmen live in splendid privacy on the top floors of the college houses. Phoebe and I stayed together three years, until custom dictated our move, as seniors, to Main Building. There the luck of the draw defeated us. I was given a room in North Tower, which was supposed to be "prestigious." Phoebe was banished to the fourth floor.

"The Advisory Board," Phoebe said now, "was because of one of those ads for a writing school. You know those ads?"

"God, yes. 'Let us tell you if you have the talent to become a published writer.' "

"You don't approve of them. I don't approve of them either. They lie to people." There was a groaning and creaking of springs. "Anyway, I was looking at one of these ads, and then I started thinking about Fires of Love. It was just after Janine asked me to do one. I'd never done a category before, but Farret was in so much trouble, and Myrra was going to do one, and I thought—"

"You thought you'd be nice." I settled a hotel ashtray on my stomach and lit a cigarette. Camille came out from under the covers, checked out the light, and turned around to go back to sleep. I said, "You're always trying to be nice."

"I keep thinking of why someone would want to blackmail everyone on the Fires of Love Advisory Board, and I can't. I mean, I can't make it make sense. There isn't anything."

"Maybe, it's something that's coming," I suggested. "They want to get you all to do something, so they set this thing up—"

"Set what up?" Phoebe said. "I wasn't being blackmailed. So what was happening?"

"I don't know," I said. I took a drag on what had to be the filter of my cigarette and stubbed it out. "Go to sleep. We'll think about it in the morning."

Phoebe sighed. "It was just a publicity stunt, a lot of famous romance writers and an agent. People would look at the ads and think, with all those people involved, it must be good. You know what I mean?"

"Yes."

"Pay?" Voice very high and strained. "Pay, do you think I'm famous?"

I thought about it. I never had before. Phoebe was always Phoebe. She rescued alley cats. She loved touristy restaurants. She had started just out of college in a third floor walk-up on the Lower East Side, complete with bathtub in the kitchen. Now there were ten rooms on Central Park West in the nineties and strand upon strand of rope diamonds. In less than ten years.

"Not as famous as Myrra," I told her. "Not yet. But getting there."

There was another creaking and groaning of springs. "Just one thing," she said, voice very small now, "I don't know what I think about it. You understand? I don't know how I'm supposed to feel about it."

"Feel happy."

"It isn't that simple."

A moment later, I heard the regular sawing whistle of her deep breathing. Phoebe was asleep.

I've always wanted to be able to fall asleep like that.

CHAPTER 23

What Phoebe said was, *"Ben Hur is waiting for you in the living room. So is Nick."*

She said it to the back of my head, which was covered by a blue, red, and gold Cathay-Pierce quilt. I was trying to recuperate from having been awakened, at nine o'clock on Sunday morning, by Nick's mother. Nick's mother was lamenting the fact that Nick was not with her, on his way to church.

"Every Sunday morning of his life," she said. "Every Tuesday and Thursday afternoon at the Greek school. He thinks he's all grown up, he stops going to church. Does this seem nice to you?"

"No," I said.

"Tell him I put a little bag in his pocket," she said. "He thinks he's all grown up, he stops eating."

"You've got to wake *up,*" Phoebe said.

I came out from under the quilt. I made my eyes focus. It didn't help. Phoebe looked like a large yellow beach ball.

"Your friend Barbara was right," Phoebe said. "It was Ben Hur. I mean, of course, not the original—"

I reached for my cigarettes, found one Camille had not shredded, and lit it. Phoebe was wearing a yellow terry cloth robe in the approximate shape of a monk's habit. That explained the beach ball.

"Nick's mother wants to know why he isn't at church," I said.

"Make sense," Phoebe said. She sat on the edge of the bed and curled her feet under her. There was nothing left of the small voice of the night before. Her eyes were bright and round. Her hair was pinned to the top of her head like a wiry, manic crown. She had been up for hours. "He's out there eating Nick's baklava," she said. "He won't talk to us. It has to be *you.* " She leaned forward and squinted into my eyes. "You think you're ready to get up yet?"

I took a drag and stared at the ceiling. Phoebe not only slept well and easily, she woke immediately. She was more coherent when she first opened her eyes than I was after six cups of coffee.

"I'll get up when you start making sense," I said. "Ben Hur. Ben Hur cannot be in the living room of a suite in the Cathay-Pierce."

"Not Ben Hur Ben Hur," Phoebe said. She got off the bed and headed for the living room. "Jaimie Hallman Ben Hur."

She had closed the door behind her when it hit me.

"For God's sake," I said. *"Phoebe.* Jaimie Hallman's *dead.* "

Jaimie Hallman was not dead. He didn't look much like the eighteen-year-old boy who'd won three gold medals in the 1960 summer Olympics in Rome. He looked even less like the too handsome young man who had been America's favorite movie star for nearly two decades after that. But he was alive, and when I first saw him, relaxed and distracted on Phoebe's blue velvet couch, he still had the fine-boned, almost delicate face of the kind of man people called "beautiful."

His presumed death had been the biggest story of 1980. It still did very good business in papers like the *National Enquirer.* It had love and death, mystery and terror—and movie stars. Some photographer had taken a picture of the boat Hallman had been sailing before his disappearance. It drifted like a ghost ship at the edges of an expensively dredged marina. The body, needless to say, had never been found.

The body had found us. It saw me and tried to get up. Something went wrong. Its arms trembled and jerked. It smiled.

"It's all this running around," he said, his voice clear and distinct. "The L-dopa only does so much."

"Mr. Hallman has been telling me why he's supposed to be dead when he isn't dead," Nick said. He used his best professional voice. It annoyed me. Trying to make things make sense was laudible. Forcing them to was ridiculous. A dead person had just walked into Phoebe's temporary living room. It was not the time or place for the American Bar Association waltz.

"Your mother called," I told him. "She wanted to know why you weren't in church."

Nick's eyes got as wild as Rasputin's. He looked ready to kick me. His mother must have made a regular practice of this sort of thing.

"About Mr. Hallman—" he started, stiff as an old maid.

"It was a mistake," Jaimie Hallman said.

"You people are terrible," Phoebe said. She threw a quilt over him, poured him a cup of something from the room service tray, and started stuffing velvet throw pillows in unlikely places. In less than a minute, Jaimie Hallman looked like a goosedown mountain with a head of blond hair sticking out of it.

He smiled at Phoebe. Then he looked at us.

"She's all right," he said. "I walk in the door, first thing I know I've got tea. I've got bagels and cream cheese and lox. I've got baklava and cookies." He looked at his lap. "Now I've got more tea, a quilt, and a cat."

"Oh, Jesus," Nick said. We both recognized the look on Jaimie Hallman's face. It was the look Marty Caine always had whenever he spoke of Phoebe. It was the look *everybody* had five minutes after they met her. You had to be a close friend before you realized she wasn't a stereotypical Jewish mother in training. Jaimie Hallman wasn't a close friend. He was physically exhausted. For the moment, he thought Phoebe was a saint.

"Mr. Hallman's been running around to your apartment for days," Phoebe said. "In his condition. He has to *rest.*"

"I can't rest," Jaimie Hallman said. "I've been trying to tell this to somebody since Friday. The police won't listen to me. You were never home."

"They sealed my apartment," I said. I didn't mention the smells of blood and urine, or my impulse to walk away from that apartment and everything now in it. I didn't want to push Jaimie Hallman any farther than I had to.

Jaimie Hallman had been pushed too far as it was. He lay his head against the back of the couch and closed his eyes. The lines were deep gouges on either side of his mouth. He looked seventy instead of forty.

"It just disappeared," he said.

"What just disappeared?" Nick and I at once.

"The knife that killed Julie. I *had* it."

I thought Nick was going to cough himself into an aneurism. He got up and started pacing the room, the great bulk of him out of control. The intensity of those movements was disturbing. It was as if he were looking for a justification for violent physical activity. Having got it, he would push himself until we were all exhausted.

It was entirely out of character, but I didn't ask what was wrong. I was edgy myself. It was Sunday morning. Things were getting too close. In a few hours, even I wouldn't be able to pretend anymore.

"Jesus H. Christ," Nick said. "*When* did you lose it? Where did you lose it?"

"It had to be before last night," I said. "Before Leslie."

"Leslie Ashe was stabbed with a hotel kitchen knife," Nick said. "Myrra and Julie were stabbed with a long, thin, double-edged blade." He stopped in mid-pace and stared at Jaimie Hallman.

Hallman stared back at us, trying to understand what was going on. Confusion made him anxious. There were creases of strain across his forehead.

"I'm sorry," Nick said. "I didn't mean to."

"I lost it this morning," he said. "In the hotel. I had it wrapped up in tissue paper. It was in my pocket when I walked into the hotel, and then it wasn't after I got in here."

"Did you talk to anyone?" I asked. "Were there people in the elevator?"

"I talked to everyone," Jaimie Hallman said. "This place is packed. To the gills. The elevator was like a subway at rush hour, except I knew everybody. Janine Williams. Hazel Ganz. Amelia Samson. Half Julie's client roster—"

"How did you know Julie?" I asked.

Jaimie Hallman's eyes widened. "I was married to her," he said. "In 1979. Just before—" He waved his trembling arm in the air. "Parkinson's disease. That was why we didn't do anything about the death reports."

"Mr. Hallman had a boating accident in 1980," Phoebe said, as if no one had ever heard of Jaimie Hallman's "drowning." "He was lost for a couple of days. He had trouble swimming."

"Beginning of this," Jaimie Hallman waved his arm again. "It was a mistake. The papers started saying I was dead. No one knew I was married to Julie. The way my money was set up, it didn't matter." He considered. "I'm not officially dead," he said, "just missing."

"That's a relief," I said.

Jaimie Hallman sighed. "It would have come out eventually. We had the baby a year and a half ago. She's got to be taken care of. I'm calling myself Jay Simms, but I think that police detective is onto it. Onto something, anyway. The whole thing was a fluke. I'm surprised it lasted this long."

"Specifics," Nick insisted. "The knife. How did you get the knife?"

"If you're thinking I killed her, forget it," Jaimie Hallman said. "These days, the best I do is get it up. Much effort beyond that, I can't make. The knife came in the mail."

"What?" Actually, three *"whats,"* in unison.

"It came in the mail," Jaimie Hallman said. "The morning after Julie was murdered. It couldn't have been sent, but my doorman didn't see anyone deliver it." He paused. "You know, it had to be pretty early in the morning. Well before nine. By eight-thirty there would have been people around—"

"Maybe there were people around," Nick said. "Maybe someone did see it delivered. Maybe—"

"After eight-thirty, we've got two doormen," Jaimie Hallman said. "Somebody's *always* at the door. Nobody saw anyone come in with a package. Nobody saw anyone they didn't know, period. Yet when I went to the package carrels, there it was. And it wasn't there Thursday."

"That doesn't mean anything," Nick shook his head. "If it was a nice, middle-class–looking white woman, no one would have noticed."

"After eight-thirty, someone would have noticed."

Nick sighed. "Was it a long, thin, double-bladed knife?"

"It was a steel-bladed, ebony- and ivory-handled machete."

"Oh, Jesus *Christ,*" Nick said.

They sat silently across from each other, looking mutually tired. Phoebe bustled. I lit another cigarette. *"It would have come out eventually,"* Jaimie Hallman had said. Something was beginning to dawn on me.

Logic is a wonderful invention. It is so wonderful, people often mistake it for reason. Reason, however, requires sense. Logic requires only consistency.

There was something very consistent about what had *not* happened to Phoebe and to Amelia Samson. If the same thing had also *not* happened to Julie Simms, I would have an explanation for at least half the nonsense I'd discovered this weekend.

"This business about being dead," I said to Jaimie Hallman, "how important was it? Would you have paid blackmail to keep it from coming out?"

Jaimie Hallman blinked. Phoebe, walking by with a small tray of amorphous pastry, kicked my ankle.

"It was a joke," Jaimie Hallman said. "There's this psychic who works for the *National Enquirer.*" He blushed. "You know those stories? Jaimie Hallman speaks from beyond the grave? They're true. I go to this psychic and—uh, appear. If you see what I mean." He gave a tentative shrug. "It keeps the residuals coming in."

"But no blackmail going out."

"None at all. It was going to come out when it came out. Lately I didn't really care. In the beginning—" He stared at his right thumb, twitching and jerking as if it was on strings. "Julie and I were pretty good together," he said finally. "She cared, but she didn't really mind. She wasn't in it for Jaimie Hallman, movie star. I think I wanted to be dead, in the beginning. She got me over it."

"Exactly," I said. "Just what I thought."

CHAPTER 24

Someone, probably the lawyers, had changed the locks on Myrra's apartment. I should have expected it. At the very least, I should have come prepared for it. Everything else was wrong, upside down, frustrating. Why shouldn't Myrra's locks be changed?

I tried my keys twice, gave up, and got out my credit cards.

"Phoebe taught me to do this," I told Nick.

He stood in the narrow back hall, arms crossed over his chest, fuming. I concentrated on the door and reminded myself it was enough that he had come. He didn't want to be here. He didn't like sneaking in the service entrance of the Braedenvorst and taking a freight elevator to the twelfth floor. It was a tribute to the lifetime influence of Phoebe Damereaux that he had agreed to this expedition.

"There are several things wrong with this," he said. "For one thing, we're breaking and entering. For another, someone may be in there. For a third—"

"I can't break in to something I own," I said. The lock jerked, wobbled, caught again. I reapplied the credit card. "We're going in the back way," I said. "It's Sunday afternoon. It'll be all right."

"It would be better if you told me what you were doing," Nick said.

The lock snapped. I turned the knob and opened the door onto another narrow back hall, the "servants' hall" in Myrra's ancient, oak-paneled apartment. I peered into the darkness. If Martinez didn't get me convicted of murder, I would own this apartment, and everything in it as of the day Myrra Agenworth died. I would have to sell the paintings and the furniture just to pay the maintenance.

I took Nick by the wrist and pulled him inside. "Think like Myrra," I told him, creeping through the hall.

He stopped. He took off his shoes. He looked—*endearing,* padding along in his socks.

"I don't know what that's supposed to mean," he said.

We went through a swinging door into a large, more expensively decorated hall. Large, dark rooms opened on either side. I stuck my head in each one. Bed followed bed. Draped damask canopy followed draped damask canopy.

"Go at it the other way around," I said. "Marian Pinckney says there were seven blackmail accounts in the New York Guaranty. One was Myrra's. One was Julie's. Of the other five, Phoebe, you and I have, individually or jointly, talked to four. I don't know about Lydia, but Amelia, Marty Caine and Jaimie Hallman definitely say there wasn't any blackmail. Phoebe and I figured it out about Janine. She didn't have the money to be paying someone a thousand dollars a month."

"So somebody's lying," Nick said.

"Not exactly."

Myrra's study was the last room on the left. I turned on the electrified brass chandelier that hung from the center of the twenty-foot ceiling. Even then, the room was dark. Blood-colored drapes covered the windows. A bloodred carpet barely covered the dark wood floor. Heavy lamps and overstuffed chairs crowded along the wall.

Myrra's desk was an ornate rosewood secretary, the kind with five or six secret drawers. Its polished wood surface had never known a typewriter. Myrra dictated her novels while lying in the heart-shaped sunken bathtub—or said she did. They all had odd places for writing or dictating: in bed, while flying, only after making love. Phoebe would have to invent something like that. It didn't do just to write at a desk.

Beside me, Nick shifted, nervous, jumpy, resentful. "If you're so smart," he said, "tell me about the knife. What was Jaimie Hallman doing with it?"

"The knife is easy," I told him. "Husbands kill wives. Just in case I didn't make it as a suspect, whoever would at least have Jaimie Hallman to take up the slack." I ran my hand along the underside of the top shelf, found a knob, and pulled. Nothing happened. I pushed. Nothing happened. "It's got to be here somewhere," I said.

"*What* does?" He sounded ready to strangle me, but I ignored him. It was Sunday afternoon. Anybody in this apartment would be breaking and entering even more surely than we were. As I continued to point out to Nick, I was at least the heir apparent.

"Think like Myrra," I told him. "Look at what you have. You've got something wrong at Fires of Love. We don't know how she found that out, but she did. There's something wrong at Fires of Love—"

"But we can't know that," Nick protested. "There isn't one thing to indicate anything's going wrong at Farret."

"Not at Farret," I said. "At Fires of Love. Fires of Love is the Advisory Board as well as the editorial and marketing staff. And we know it's Fires of Love because of the blackmail list. Phoebe figured that out yesterday. Last night. Whenever. At any rate, think like Myrra. You're a fanatic about business honesty. You want to get this person, only you're not exactly sure who it is, and you don't have any way to find out. Maybe you know it's nothing illegal, just unethical. Maybe it's illegal, but you don't know how it's being done, or you can't prove it. Whatever it is, it can't be corrected through normal channels. Being Myrra, you'd use normal channels if you could."

"Being me, I'd use normal channels if I could," Nick said drily.

"All right," I said. "But you're Myrra. And you can't use normal channels. For some reason, this time that won't work. Whoever it is, is going to get away. But you won't let them. The idea infuriates you. Any one of these seven people could have done it, and when you find out who it is, you're going to get them. Good."

"So you blackmail seven people, *including yourself?*"

"No, no," I said. "You don't blackmail anybody. You're Myrra, remember. You'd never do anything like that."

"Somebody did something," Nick said. "There are seven live accounts wandering around."

"I know," I said. "But nobody blackmailed anybody. We haven't found one person who admits to being blackmailed."

"Exactly." Nick raised a single finger. "Who admits to it."

"Phoebe is not being blackmailed," I said. "If Phoebe is not being blackmailed, and money's going in and out of her account anyway, then that's probably what's happening to the rest of the accounts. Or do you think somebody's paying Phoebe's blackmail for her?"

Nick shook his head. "No," he said. "I do not think someone is paying Phoebe's blackmail for her. That would be a bit much, even for Phoebe."

I smiled, meaning to blither about Phoebe, our only neutral subject. Then my hand hit something under the second shelf. I ran my fingers along the rough edge of a peg, then pushed it slowly, carefully toward the back of the cabinet.

A door in the cabinet's face sprung open like a jack-in-the-box.

Plastic cards cascaded down to the lacquered writing surface.

Leslie Ashe, edging into the room through the double doors from the sitting room, said,

"Oh, bloody *hell.*"

CHAPTER 25

Leslie Ashe had not been cut on the face. Her right arm was in a sling, her left arm had bandages to the wrist, and she looked pale, but she hadn't been cut on the face. I tried to remember who had told me that she had been, but I couldn't. I was too distracted by the fact that Leslie Ashe was nothing at all like Gamble Daere.

Leslie Ashe and Gamble Daere were the same person. I knew that. Their features were identical. Gamble Daere, however, was a flake. It was in the way she stood, the way she moved. Leslie Ashe was a healthy, stolid, almost clumsy English girl of the kind fond of walking tours. Her face was scrubbed clean of makeup. Her hair was pulled into a ponytail. Her head was firmly planted on her neck.

I wanted to congratulate her on having managed so complete a transformation. If I had been sure of her good will, I would have. Instead, I stood back to let her look over my shoulder at the plastic cards on the desk.

She said, "Oh."

"Oh shit would be more like it," I said.

"They won't tell you anything," she said. "I tried. I can't see Aunt Myrra—" She said "aunt" with an "ah," the way we do in Connecticut. Phoebe says "ant."

"I can't see Myrra, either," I said. "I don't think she did. I don't think anybody blackmailed anybody."

We nodded gravely to each other.

"Nobody blackmailed or everybody blackmailed," Leslie said. "One thing makes as much sense as the other."

"Would somebody please tell me what's going on?"

We both looked at Nick and blinked. He seemed unnecessarily

wrought up, as if he was responding to a calamity neither Leslie nor I could see. We were caught in our speculations, as if speculations were all that mattered. We had known Myrra. We were united in having known Myrra.

I reminded myself I did not know Leslie Ashe. She could have come from England to murder Myrra. I didn't believe it—she seemed too ruthlessly sensible for that—but she stood to inherit ten times the value of the apartment. She would have good reason to frame me too. If I were convicted of Myrra's murder, I would not be allowed to inherit the apartment. It would revert to the DeFord estate, and to Leslie herself.

I turned my attention to Nick. He was still confused, and beginning to look angry.

"Nobody blackmailed anybody," I said. "Myrra set up the accounts. Myrra made up Amelia's envelope, and probably others. Myrra deposited the money and took it out."

"Whatever for?" Nick put his head in his hands. Wiry tufts of black hair stuck through the spaces between his fingers. "Why in the name of God would anyone—"

"To get back at someone," Leslie said. "To catch someone. I hadn't thought of that." She nodded vigorously. "I'll have to tell Teri about that. It's the first thing that's made any sense since we got here."

"Who's Teri?" I asked.

Leslie blushed. "The blond woman," she said. "The one the other day at the conference. I didn't mean to cause you a lot of trouble—"

"You just wanted to get the blackmail envelope out of your hands," I said. "Did you find it here?"

"With the cards. And a list of secret numbers. Julie Simms never had it, of course. I just needed a reason to give it to you . . ." She shuffled her feet against the floor. "I tried to use Myrra's card in the machine," she said, "but the numbers weren't labeled, and it didn't work." She tugged at the sling on her arm, frowning. "I've been over everything in the apartment. I've been over Myrra's royalty statements and those computer reports they send her. I've read her mail. I haven't found anything."

"It couldn't be royalty statements," I said. "Myrra knew royalty statements. She could read a printout at two hundred yards."

"You're running on the assumption that Aunt Myrra got killed because she found out who was doing whatever?" Leslie asked. I nodded. "Okay," she said, "why'd it take her nine months?"

We made a list of everything that had happened in November that might or might not have tipped Myrra off to *who* was doing *what.* We made a list of everything that might have alerted someone to the fact that Myrra was investigating whatever they were doing. We made a list of everything that could have gone wrong at Fires of Love. Leslie made coffee in Myrra's barn-sized kitchen. Nick passed out baklava. None of us got anywhere.

"We've got to assume Myrra knew *what,*" Leslie said. "Or approximately what."

"We'd better say approximately," Nick said. He rescued a silver coffee spoon from Camille, who was trying to drag it into my tote bag. He picked her up and held her against his chest. "We can't think of one damn thing all seven of these people are capable of."

"As applied to Fires of Love," I said.

"As applied to Fires of Love," he agreed. "Let's do this another way." He turned to Leslie. "Let's look at last night. You told Martinez it couldn't have been Pay who stabbed you."

"A small person," Leslie said. "Smaller than I am. Head came up to about my shoulder. I'm five ten."

"Mary Allard," I said. "Amelia."

"Possibly Mary Allard," Leslie said. "Not Amelia. I'd have known if it was someone that fat. It could have been Teri, except I think I would have recognized Teri. And she was supposed to be on her way out of town."

"Could it have been a man?" I asked. "Marty Caine?"

"It could have been Marty Caine. Or Janine Williams. Or Phoebe Damereaux." I blanched, but she didn't notice. "It could have been that girl, the one who's always lecturing people about contracts and pseudonyms—"

"Hazel Ganz," I said.

"Hazel Ganz. I didn't get a chance to see anything. I walked in, I put my hand on the light switch, and the next I remember there were police. The room was all torn up. I don't remember it *happening.*"

Nick put cream in the blue china saucer to his coffee cup, put Camille down beside it, and watched her drink. He was beginning to get shadows under his eyes and fine red lines on his nose.

"Why did you go up there in the first place?" he asked.

Leslie shrugged. "I don't know. I thought something might be there. I—well, I still thought Myrra was blackmailing people. It didn't make sense, but I did. And Janine Williams and Marty Caine were two of them."

"Mary Allard knew you were going up there," I said. "Why tell her? She rode up in the elevator with you."

"And kept riding," Leslie insisted. "And I didn't really tell anyone. They've got a lot of Myrra's books in the Farret suite. I said I wanted to go up and get them."

"Said to who?" Nick asked.

"Oh, a whole lot of people. Amelia Samson was buying drinks. There was a table full of people from the conference. Everybody we've been talking about but Phoebe, I guess."

We stared at each other, tired, depressed, hopeless. Camille stepped in her cream and made tracks across the table. I lit a cigarette and watched the light fade outside the kitchen window. There comes a point when you can't think anymore, and I was past it.

I was also due at the AWR Cocktail Reception, in the Starlit Room of the Cathay-Pierce, at seven-thirty. So was Leslie. So was Nick.

So was Mary Allard, who had been the first person to realize that the knife used on Leslie Ashe was not the knife used on Julie or Myrra.

CHAPTER 26

If I hadn't been preoccupied, I would have noticed. Instead, I was busy with Nick—a Nick who seemed to have undergone a sea change in the short cab ride across the park. He left me to pay the cab driver while he headed into the Cathay-Pierce at a near run. He glared at the women waiting for elevators as if they had personally offended him. He pushed me into a crowded car as if he was forcing meat into a sausage casing. Approached by Janine, by Marty Caine, by Hazel Ganz—by everyone I or Phoebe had introduced him to at the conference—he stared resolutely at the ceiling. I stared at the ceiling, too. The atmosphere in that elevator was so foul, I was afraid to inhale.

When we got to the suite, he marched through the living room, closed himself in Phoebe's bedroom, and started making phone calls. Phoebe watched him go with a shrug.

"What happened?" she asked me.

I told her. I told her everything, up to and including the scene in the elevator. Then I settled back to watch Camille try to steal the couch. Camille was making a habit of stealing, though she preferred objects small enough to hide in my tote bag.

Phoebe paced the carpet, stopped, paced again, stopped. She stared through the bedroom door at Nick hunched over the phone.

"It doesn't make sense," she said. "Nothing happened. He only gets that way when things are totally *fubar.*" She considered. "Maybe worse."

"Things are the same as they always were," I said, "except that Myrra was doing God knows what, for God knows what reason. And I don't know how to separate Myrra's nonsense from what's really important."

"Concentrate on your apartment," Phoebe said.

I concentrated instead on getting ready for the cocktail party. I took a very long shower under a needle-hard spray and thought of nothing, not even home and Connecticut and my Christmas stocking. I put on black satin evening pajamas. I gave my hair five hundred strokes with a wire brush. I sat down at the vanity table for a nice long session with my makeup.

My sessions with makeup are always long. I wear it only when I must also wear evening dress, so I have no idea what to do with it. I stare at the mirror and draw and dab. I let myself drift and forget what I'm doing. I dream.

This time I dreamed my favorite dream: I am sitting up in a large bed, a dozen feather pillows propped behind my back. The sheets are starched white Irish linen. The quilt that covers them is goosedown. On the night table to my right is a glass of Bailey's Old Irish Cream liqueur. In my hands is a country house murder or a good ghost story. Outside it is snowing.

I could go on like that forever.

I had tried and rejected three different faces when Nick came in, looking haggard and furious. The odd intensity of mood I had first noticed in him this morning was still with him. It seemed to have neither direction nor release.

"I was off the phone for *one second,*" he said. "Amelia Samson called."

"What did she want?"

"How am I supposed to know? I told her you were out."

He tramped back to the bedroom. I followed him, my face slicked over with cold cream. I found him sitting on the edge of the bed, hunched over the phone like a gambler with a double or nothing on a long shot.

He hung up a few moments later. I was sitting on the far side of the room, smoking a cigarette and staring at his back, but he didn't turn around.

"That apartment," he said. "I didn't realize how much trouble we were in until I saw that apartment. I called Martinez."

"What did he say?" The idea of Nick talking to Martinez made me queasy. It called up visions of peace talks and generals and two nations searching for an honorable way to end the war. I didn't want to end this particular war.

"We can't bargain," Nick said. "I knew that. Now I know I *know* that."

"I don't want to bargain."

He didn't answer. My words floated in the silence, stinging my eyes like smoke. I'd spent twenty-four hours treating Nick Carras like a cardboard dress-up doll, suitable for carrying doped-up romance writers through hotel hallways and breaking into sealed apartments, and now he was sitting with his back to me. My one defense against Martinez. The one person who both wished me well and could *do* something about it.

I started thinking about my parents, my niece and nephews, my brother and sister-in-law. I hadn't even called them since all this started. I hadn't shopped for Christmas presents.

I was too tired to think. I was disintegrating into irrationality. It was ridiculous to think I was falling in love with a man I had not only met the day before, but not bothered to notice until the last five minutes. I said, "I didn't kill Julie Simms. I didn't kill Myrra."

"I know that." Now he turned to face me, but he didn't leave the bed. I thought crazily that he didn't want to come too close to a murderess.

"Martinez has been working all weekend," he said. "So has the district attorney's office. They're going to bring you before a grand jury next week. Maybe even tomorrow. And they're going to get an indictment."

"An indictment isn't everything."

"If we went to trial tomorrow, you'd be convicted."

"We aren't going to trial tomorrow." Now the tears were really close, the tears and the tiredness. I wanted to curl up in a dark closet with a blanket and the cat. "We'll have months and months," I said. "A lot of time."

"We'll have our fingerprints all over Myrra Agenworth's apartment. All over her desk. All over her private papers." He sighed. "We shouldn't have done that."

"Why not?" I asked him. "We can't just sit around doing nothing. Martinez isn't even looking for alternatives."

"I know he isn't. But you didn't kill Julie Simms, and you didn't kill Myrra, and he has to prove his case. We've got the time factor."

"Murder suspects don't get out on bail," I said. "They won't let me go to Connecticut for Christmas."

"McKenna—"

We both knew I was being unreasonable. I knew he was trying to give me good advice. I didn't want to hear it. I got up and headed for the dressing room.

"You ought to start getting dressed," I told him. "We're due downstairs any minute."

"McKenna."

I shut the door of the dressing room. I sat at the vanity mirror and looked at my eyes. Puffy and red—even the threat of tears does that to me. It was so odd to feel frightened and resentful at once. The fear made me want to throw myself in his arms. The resentment—*why* couldn't we conduct an independent investigation? *why* couldn't we come up with our own solution?—made me want to kill him.

I pulled my tote bag into my lap. It was full of lipstick cases and rouge bottles, dragged there by Camille, who protested their removal by digging her nails into my fingers. I took her out and put her on the table, where she started worrying one of Phoebe's sterling silver compacts. Then I started searching for my eye shadow.

I was on my third try when I felt them. There was a bent prong. I nicked my finger.

I pulled my hand out and stared at the blood. I could not possibly have known what cut me, but I did. I truly did. It figured.

There was a knock on the door and Nick said, "I didn't mean to upset you."

"I'm all right," I said. "I'll only be a minute."

I put my hands in the tote bag again. I found the prong. I got my fingers around the metal.

Myrra's ruby key ring winked and glittered in the light of the soft-white bulbs that surrounded the vanity mirror.

Myrra's ruby key ring. The one with the keys to my apartment, the one she was carrying the night she died. What would Martinez think of that?

The keys to her apartment were sterling silver, custom-made at Tiffany's. The keys to my apartment were tin and red.

They lay against my hand like blood.

CHAPTER 27

I didn't tell Nick about the keys. I let him escort me downstairs, look-ing stiff and nervous in his dinner jacket, and sent him for champagne as soon as we got into the Starlit Room. I wanted to be rid of him. I needed to talk to Phoebe.

I should have known better. The Starlit Room was lit by thousands and thousands of candles screwed into chandeliers, carefully positioned to shed the least possible light while presenting the greatest possible danger to the red-and-white crepe paper streamers hung from every wall, window, and table. In the center of the room a red-and-white iced cake, made in the shape of a heart and the size of a dining room table, stood ready for the Queen of Court and her Prince Charming to pop out of. Prince Charming was a low-level mafioso with a weak chin and sunglasses. The Queen of Court, chosen by lottery, was a comfortably padded woman from Lansing, Michigan, with a passion for Barbara Cartland.

What it was supposed to be was a Grand Ball. What it was was a Senior Prom without boys. Even the oldest women wore ruffled, pastel chiffons. Several wore very pale pink makeup favored by mothers for their sweet sixteen daughters. The band played the "Theme from Mondo Cane." Over and over again.

A woman in bright pink hair and a lime green dress came by carrying a cardboard box covered with pink tissue paper.

"*Miss* McKenna," she said. "May I have your *pink* voting card, please."

I rummaged in my bag, disturbing Camille's nap, and found a pink envelope with a heart and arrow printed in one corner. BALLOT, it read. QUEEN OF HEARTS. The Queen of Hearts is what the American Writers of Romance call their president. I passed over Lydia and Amelia and wrote in Phoebe's name.

"There," I said, stuffing it into the ballot box.

The woman sniffed. She turned on her heel and walked off, calling for pink voting cards.

I wandered away. It was impossible to see anything clearly. It was impossible to know who was speaking or where they were.

"I told my agent I *would not* take less than seven thousand for the new book," someone said, "and this time I want *ninety*—"

"The tip sheet makes it sound as if the line's going to be one long sex scene with props, but she's got to be a virgin until the very last *page*, practically, so how—"

Somebody grabbed my arm and spun me around.

"Unions," Hazel Ganz barked at me, her breath sweet and hot with the smell of champagne. "What about unions?"

"I don't know," I said.

"You have to know," Hazel Ganz said. "*Longshoremen* could form a union. *Musicians* could form a union. Even *actors* could form a union. Thirty years from now, when we're eating cabbage and cat food in welfare hotels, we'll be able to congratulate ourselves on having been perfect little ladies."

She whirled away into the darkness.

"There you are," Janine said. "Phoebe's got a dog. We've been looking all over for you."

She drew me into a little group consisting of Phoebe with Esmeralda in her arms, Marty Caine already drunk, and Amelia and Lydia, each with cardboard campaign posters. Amelia's had her sitting at a Chippendale desk, making a poor attempt at quiet dignity. Lydia's showed her borne aloft on the shoulders of a million Japanese.

"The Far Eastern tour," Lydia said, waving her overpainted nails in the air. "Do you know I'm the second bestselling author in Japan?"

"I'm sure," Amelia said, "it has something to do with the fact that they can't read English."

"I was there for all of September," Lydia said. "I signed so many books, my right hand had to be put in a *cast.*"

"Don't be silly," Janine said. "You're left-handed."

Lydia glared. Amelia took a great breath and shouted, "It is my considered opinion that the results of this election will determine the course of romance writing for this century."

"Oh God," Phoebe said. "They've been doing this for *hours*. Now Lydia will say—"

"There's an entirely new *thrust* in the romance genre." Lydia's eyes glittered. Her hand came out of her bag waving a brown plastic pill bottle. She popped two yellow jackets and washed them down with champagne.

"The entire *point* of romance," Amelia said, throwing back her arms and hitting me in the side, "is that love is more than the satiation of instincts most accurately described as *base.*"

"*Savage Breath of Love,*" Lydia said. "Two million copies sold."

"*The Whispered Promise,*" Amelia said. "Three and a half million copies sold."

"The Holy Bible," Phoebe waved her champagne glass in the air. "*Fifty* million copies sold." They stared at her, and she shrugged. "Maybe a hundred. Who's counting?"

She put her glass under Esmeralda's nose and let the dog drink. Esmeralda sneezed. Phoebe took the glass, downed the contents, and grabbed another from a passing tray. It occurred to me that I had only once seen her with a drink in her hand, and that had been mostly water. I had certainly never seen her drunk. I wondered what it would be like, carrying a half-crocked Phoebe to her room while she extolled the marketability of the Holy Bible.

I didn't have time to think about it. First, Janine, thrown off balance by the press of the crowd, pitched into me, hitting my tote bag broadside. Then the cat started screeching and tearing. I cut myself on something trying to get her out, and just as I was putting her in the pocket of my shirt, the candles went out.

I don't know how they went out, but they did, all at once. The only light in the room came from the dais, from what looked like a gigantic beach ball covered with Fourth of July sparklers. On closer inspection, the ball became a heart, very fatty and in danger of breaking. Nick was standing directly under it.

"Ladies and gentlemen," someone said. I supposed it was Miriam Schaff, the present Queen of Hearts, who wrote Regencies under the name Emalaya Marchband. "Welcome to the Third Annual Conference of the American Writers of Romance."

The crowd applauded, and someone shouted, "Next year on Valentine's Day!"

That got more applause. I started pushing through, heading for Nick.

"We open this conference at the end of the most successful year in the history of romance publishing," Miriam Schaff said. "A year of great gains in variety, creativity, and respect. A year when we have proved, once and for all, that romance writing and romance writers are the mainstream of fiction in this country."

The applause was wild, loud, frightening. I stumbled over someone's foot and fell into Nick.

"My God," Nick said as he caught me. "What's going *on* here? Is everybody crazy?"

"Have you ever seen Phoebe drink before?" I asked him.

"What?"

"Drink." I waved vaguely at the crowd. "She keeps swallowing whole glasses of champagne. She feeds them to the dog."

Nick turned a little green. "Oh, *no,*" he said.

"That's what I was afraid of," I said. I pushed away from him into the crowd, thinking I should have stopped and told him about the keys. I should have told him before, because now there wasn't time. I had to find Phoebe and get her away from the champagne before there was a disaster.

"The Queen of Hearts," Miriam Schaff said, "is the most important position in this organization. She is the most important woman among us. She is the recipient of our highest honor. For the past year, I have had the great good fortune to occupy that position among you."

I found a piece of wall and leaned against it. The crowd was pressing forward, waiting, eager. It would be impossible to break through them.

It was better to sit back and wait for the results of the election, then catch Phoebe when the lights went on.

"On the ballot tonight," Miriam Schaff said, "are two women whose contributions to the romance genre have been inestimable. Amelia Samson's novels have brought comfort and hope to millions of women in America, Europe, and Asia. Lydia Wentward has changed the very face of our landscape, opening new and exciting areas for exploration."

"And new and exciting ways of exploring them, too," someone behind me said.

"But you have seen fit to choose neither of these fine women as your Queen." The crowd settled down. "In an unprecedented move, you have chosen a third, a woman whose name is not on the ballot, a woman who has been among us a shorter time than most, but whose work has brought great honor to our profession. She did not ask for this honor, but I am sure she will accept it with all the graciousness of her most gracious nature.

"Ladies and gentlemen, may I present your new Queen of Hearts, the woman who symbolizes for this organization and for all the world the high professional standards and the deeply felt moral commitment of the American Writers of Romance.

"Miss Phoebe Damereaux."

The lights went on. Phoebe, caught in the exact center of the room in midgulp, spluttered. Amelia and Lydia looked shellshocked. Leslie Ashe looked happy. Janine handed Phoebe a fresh drink. Phoebe drank it.

"Wonderful," somebody beside me said. "I just voted for her because I like her books."

"What else were you supposed to do?" somebody else said. "With those two battleaxes going after each other tooth and claw, it was embarrassing."

Phoebe bobbed into the air on the shoulders of Amelia Samson and four of the wrens. She reached into her pockets, came out with a fist of halvah, and threw it into the crowd. Somebody handed her another drink, and she drank it. Somebody else, closer to the dais, handed her yet another, and she drank that, too. Amelia and the wrens put her on the stage. Someone came by with a third pink champagne. I began pushing through the crowd.

"Oh," Phoebe said into the microphone. "Oh, this is wonderful. I never expected *this.*" She wobbled. "Thank you," she said. "And especially thank Myrra, even if she couldn't be here. And I'll try to live up to it. And all that. Where's Pay?"

"I'm here," I called.

"I don't think I've ever felt so wonderful," she said. "I want to thank everyone who's ever done anything for me, but it would take too long. Isn't it funny? I write these two-hundred-thousand-word books and now I can't think of anything to say. Pay? Where are you?"

"I'm here," I called again. I had to step on Hazel Ganz's foot to get to the dais. I did it gladly.

"Well," Phoebe said, "I would like to reaffirm the motto of this organization. I, too, am *dedicated to the proposition that love conquers all.*"

That was the kicker. I got to her half a second before she passed out.

CHAPTER 28

Mary Allard was the closest to us. I pushed Phoebe into her arms.

"Bathroom," I said. "Now."

She nodded, all editorial efficiency, the kind that makes you wonder why these people always lose your manuscripts, misplace the galley approval clause in your contracts, and forget to mail your checks. She took the arms, I took the feet, and we got Phoebe through the crowd and into the hall with a minimum of interference and a maximum of good-natured (I hoped) ridicule. It was hard to tell what was going on. *Newsweek* had two reporters in that room. CBS had a videotape machine.

We made it into the ladies' room, across the red-carpeted lounge, and halfway through the stall area without incident. Phoebe woke up almost as soon as she hit the tile floor.

"Patience?" she said. "Do I have food poisoning?"

"You have two and a half bottles of champagne," I said.

"And tomorrow I'll have a hangover," she said solemnly.

She got to her feet, stood over the bowl, and closed the door in my face. I went back to the lounge to join Mary Allard, who was stretched out on a violently purple couch smoking a cigarette.

"She all right?"

"As well as can be expected," I said. I reached into my tote bag, searching for cigarettes. I felt the nick, pulled back, and went hunting again. That time I felt the blade.

I took my hand out of the bag and started stroking Camille in my pocket. Not papers this time, I thought. Not photographs. Not another set of practically perfect blackmail material. Camille was biting my fingers. I must have had the smell of the thing all over my hand.

I had decided to take it out of my tote bag, Mary or no Mary, when the door slammed open and Amelia walked in, followed by a flock of wrens in pastel blue chiffon.

"Where is she?" Amelia demanded.

Mary and I both pointed lazily toward the inner room.

Amelia clumped and the wrens tittered past us. A moment later I heard Amelia say, "Miss Damereaux. You are ignoring your responsibilities as Queen of Hearts."

"Where is she?" Lydia tottered in with a joint between her teeth. "They have the crown all ready and rose petals—"

"Forgot the water vials," Janine said, piling in. "I told them to put water vials on the stems and now—"

"People are rioting," Hazel Ganz said, looking frumpy and exasperated. "Man waiting outside. Looks furious."

Janine tried casting her eyes to heaven and found only Mary Allard. Her mouth twisted into a sucking-lemons scowl. *"Booksellers,"* she said venomously.

"We've got to hurry," Leslie Ashe said, stumbling in. She marched to the inner room, and the rest of them trailed behind her. Amelia exhorted Phoebe to put aside self-indulgent childishness and rise to the dignity of her position. Lydia offered to give everyone "a little snort," and Leslie took her up on it.

I waited until I was sure they were all thoroughly occupied. Then I picked up my tote bag and carried it across the lounge to the couch where Mary had been lying. No one standing in the inner room could see me. No one coming into the lounge from outside could fail to give me ample warning.

It was just as well.

What was in the bottom of my bag was an ivory and ebony-handled, stainless steel-bladed machete, completely covered in dried and crusted blood.

"She wants you," Amelia said.

I jumped. The knife was in my hand, lying flat against the seat of the couch, hidden from Amelia by the stretch of my legs. I let it fall out of my fingers.

"Come on," Amelia said. "She wants you."

The outside door slammed open and Marty Caine appeared, his eyes wide, his hair a boiling mass of wires.

"Where is she?" he said. "They're livid out there. That dog's running amok and it's eating the daisy chain."

"If Miss McKenna wouldn't mind sparing us a moment of her time, we'd be all ready," Amelia said.

I got up. The knife was lodged in a gap between the couch cushions. I didn't think either Hazel or Amelia had seen it.

I walked across the lounge to the tiled inner room, forcing myself through the crowd to the stall where I'd left Phoebe. I caught Mary Allard's eye and shook my head.

"Phoebe?" I knocked on the closed door. "It's me, Pay."

"Are you alone?"

"Just a minute."

I looked around the room, shrugging in embarrassment. Everyone looked back. Then Lydia leaned over, finished the line of cocaine she had laid out on the stainless steel shelf beneath the mirrors, took a deep breath and announced, "All right now. Let's get ourselves together and *get out.*"

They trooped out like a flock of baby lambs—and installed themselves in the outer lounge.

Phoebe pushed the door open and peered out.

"I've been an idiot," she said.

"You've been fine." I leaned over to help her from the floor. "Let's get fixed up, now. They're all waiting to see you crowned."

She got to her feet. "I think I'm fine," she said. "I don't even feel a little bit drunk."

"You shouldn't. There isn't an ounce of alcohol in your body. Or anything else, for that matter."

She wrinkled her nose at me. Then she went to the mirror, washed the makeup off her face, and calmly and systematically put it all back on.

"Are you all right?" She squinted at my image in the mirror. "You look—strange."

"I'm fine," I said. "You probably think everything is strange. Just now. If you see what I mean."

"I don't think so," Phoebe said. "All I have to worry about is Amelia killing me."

"I'm not going to kill you," Amelia said from the other room. "Not as long as you hurry *up.*"

Everyone laughed. Phoebe straightened her back, held the sides of her caftan as if she were holding a train, and marched into the outer room.

"If I'd *known* I was going to be elected," she said. "I would not have chosen this occasion for my first experiment with alcohol."

"My God," Mary Allard groaned. "Half an hour and she's talking like Amelia already."

"Half an hour more and she'll be talking like Lydia," Janine said. "Let's get out there. Are you coming, Pay?"

"Just a minute." I leaned over the couch, picked up my bag, and ran my hand through the crack between the cushions. I extracted a Bic pen —not mine—from Camille's clutches. I made a thorough search of my tote bag. There were a number of unfamiliar-feeling objects in there, victims of Camille's escalating kleptomania, but none of them was an ivory and ebony-handled, stainless steel-bladed machete.

That seemed to have disappeared.

CHAPTER 29

I would have panicked sooner if it hadn't been for the daisy chain. The daisy chain was actually two forty-pound cylinders of daisies, one for each side of the aisle Phoebe had to march up to be crowned Queen of Hearts. The chains were held up by sixteen girls in virgin-white, sweet sixteen gowns. Esmeralda had attached herself to one of these young women. Nick had attached himself to Esmeralda. The young woman was torn between near panic at the impending ruin of her dress and the effort required for nonstop eyelash batting.

"Just let her go," I said. "You're making her think it's a game. She's loving it."

I decided that was suitably ambiguous and started to drift away. Nick held on to me.

"Just a minute," he said. "Where's Phoebe?"

I pointed vaguely to the back of the room. "Getting ready to come in. She's supposed to march in all alone, of course—"

"Of course?"

"They never have escorts for these things."

"Of course."

He dropped Esmeralda and she dropped the girl's dress. The girl looked at me, looked at Nick, looked back at me, and knelt down to pet the nice doggy. It gave me an obscure feeling of satisfaction.

"I've been chasing around after you for the past fifteen minutes," Nick said. "One minute you're here, the next you're gone. You're *all* gone. The whole batch of you."

"Get out of the way," I said, pushing him into the darkness. "It's starting."

The lights went out. The band began "Bewitched, Bothered, and

Bewildered." The great double doors at the back opened and Phoebe walked in, holding a spray of baby's breath and lavender. Behind her came the Queen of Court and her Prince, carrying roses. Behind them the girls of the daisy chain began marching up the aisle from the back.

I peered into the darkness, trying to find Amelia or Lydia or Janine or anyone I knew. Instead I found a small girl of five or six, a straw basket of rose petals in her arms, struggling onto the dais. She crossed in front of the crowd and stood solemnly beside Miriam Schaff, who put her hand down and patted the child's head. Then Phoebe reached the dais, and Miriam leaned down to help her up beside the microphone.

"Phoebe Damereaux, do you accept your election as Queen of Hearts of this assembly?"

"I do," Phoebe said.

Something moved at the back of the stage, something very slight, very quick. I strained against Nick, trying to see. Whatever it was moved again. I started inching toward it, hoping Nick would think I was trying to get a better look at the proceedings. There was so much *stuff* up there, lights and microphones and the band's equipment. Miriam was placing the gold-plated scepter with its heart-shaped head and red and white streamers in Phoebe's hand. Phoebe took it and stepped back. Miriam leaned over and came up with a single rose.

"Do you accept this rose, symbol of the undying power and beauty of the love between a man and a woman?"

"I do," Phoebe said. She took the rose. She now had something in each hand, and I knew from experience the ceremony wasn't half over.

Miriam reached up and took the crown from her own head. It was a quasireplica of the English one, with a heart where the cross should be, and it was solidly encrusted with roses. It looked like the Crown of Thorns would have if it had been subjected to Miracle Gro and a good watering.

"I present to you this crown, given to me by the first Queen of Hearts by her own hand, to wear in the hour of your glory, and to pass on to your successors."

Phoebe seemed unsure of what to do. Then she noticed the small, square, purple velvet pillow on the floor and knelt down on it, like Anne Boleyn at her beheading. I noticed the cameraman from *Newsweek* edging up to the stage.

"Accept you this crown?" Miriam Schaff said.

"I do," Phoebe said.

Miriam placed it on Phoebe's head. It slipped over Phoebe's ear. Phoebe put her hands up and fixed it.

"Rise then," Miriam Schaff said. "All hail the new Queen of Hearts."

"Long live the new Queen of Hearts," everyone said.

Phoebe looked them all over for a moment, saw me standing just beneath her, and winked. Then she turned and marched slowly and solemnly to the throne, turned again, and sat down. Somebody set off a champagne cork. Somebody else lit a sparkler. Then the lights came on, and I saw her.

Mary Allard was at the back of the stage, caught in the wires.

I didn't stop to think. Mary Allard had no business back there. Nobody but the electricians did.

I yelled, "Nick," before I realized he wasn't anywhere near me. I was already half onto the stage, stumbling over Miriam, tripping on wires and cables, upsetting the singer's microphone in the middle of the first chorus of "What the World Needs Now Is Love, Sweet Love." There was light for the first five feet and then nothing, not even shadows, just blackness. Behind me, Nick was yelling, "McKenna! McKenna! Where are you going?"

"Maybe it's the dog," somebody else said.

I saw a door, one of those heavy metal fire doors, and went through it. It was pitch-black still, but I knew where I was—in one of those back corridors hotel guests never see, used for deliveries and hiding the heating pipes and scrimping on the painting when the money gets low. I moved close to the wall and began to inch along it, listening to the sounds of footsteps coming from every side. Footsteps going up, footsteps going down. I stopped, trying to concentrate.

Not one set of footsteps, but two. A woman's shoes on metal. Other shoes, indeterminate, on wood.

I left the wall and began to move slowly, quietly, into the oropless blackness. The woman's footsteps stopped, tapped, were silent altogether. The others shuffled and dragged.

She can't hurt me, I told myself. There are a thousand people out there. She wouldn't hurt me.

I reached out and touched metal. It was the wrought iron banister of a staircase, and as I ran my hand along it, I realized the stairs themselves were made of iron. My eyes had adjusted to the darkness, but it was difficult to see more than shapes. I put my foot out and found the bottom stair, testing, groping. I put my hand out and felt along the risers, tracing the curve of the circular slope, sliding my fingers through the first thin rivulets of blood.

I was still at the bottom of those stairs when Nick arrived with a policeman, a hotel security guard, and a flashlight. As soon as they got there, I held my hands up to the light, staring a little dully at the red smeared across them.

"Jesus Christ," Nick said. "Are you all right? What were you doing? What's going on?"

"Up there," I pointed. "There's someone up there."

"Who?"

"I don't know."

They pushed past me, their shoes slapping and ringing against the metal. A few seconds later I heard Nick say, "My God."

That was all. They came down again, moving slowly. Nick was white. The hotel security guard, who looked like a man whose retirement moonlight had been soured forever, was green.

"Have you any idea what's up there?" Nick said.

"I have not been up there," I said.

"Don't go." He knelt down beside me, taking my face in his hands. He was trying to be sympathetic. He was clumsy, but he was sincere. In another time and place I might have accepted him gladly. Just then I was frightened to accept anything at all. It was so hopeless.

"We're going to have to call in some heavy police," he said. "You'd better tell me the whole thing."

I looked away, up the stairs. It wasn't just hopeless, it was absurd. "I'll tell you," I sighed. "But you won't believe me."

CHAPTER 30

There was a man from the Manhattan district attorney's office: a short, frightened, skinny man in a shiny brown suit with the frenetic air of the incurably lazy. Not one of the star performers, this one. Not a rising light of aggressive overcompetence on his way to the United States Senate. He was just a man, a flack, an assistant district attorney. He was three years younger than I was and looked at least ten years older.

He was also Detective Martinez's dream boss. The man simply wasn't there.

Martinez's partner also wasn't there. He'd never been good for anything but spouting statistics, and now he spouted too many of them, in order of what he considered importance.

Mary Allard had died, probably within the hour, probably of knife wounds. There were nine visible knife wounds in her face, neck, and chest.

She had been killed where she was found, on a landing at the top of a circular utility staircase meant as access to fuse boxes and heating ducts lodged in the ceiling.

No purse or briefcase had been found with the body.

No jewelry had been found with the body.

No money had been found with the body.

Body was discovered by Nicholas George Carras (attorney), Howard Elsen Roth (hotel security personnel), and Sergeant Thomas Belgaddio (NYPD) at 10:43 P.M.

Miss Patience Campbell McKenna (writer) was found near the scene in apparent emotional distress.

Apparent murder weapon, ebony-handled machete with steel blade approximately five inches long, was found lodged in the victim's throat.

I would say he saved the best for last, except he didn't bother to report the best at all.

The circular staircase was one of those latticework arrangements. Mary's blood was dripping down from the top, falling over the risers, staining my hands.

I just sat at the bottom with my eyes closed and my arms folded across my chest, trying to breathe. It was hard to do with Nick staring at me, still furious after my recital of "the story" from the point when I'd found Myrra's keys to the death of Mary. It was even harder when I thought of that knife. If somebody hadn't wiped it clean, my fingerprints were going to be all over it.

Which would give Martinez just the opening he needed.

Nick sat beside me, his body so rigid that if I'd flicked a fingernail against him, he'd have come apart like a sheet of ice. I had told him, and he had believed me. He had also stopped talking to me. I was a lemming, he said. I wanted to commit suicide.

"Don't say anything," he hissed in my ear. *"Don't say one word."*

"There's nothing I can say," I told him. "I didn't even know who was dead until you told me."

"Not here," he said. "We will hold this discussion at a more suitable time and place. Better yet, you can hold it with your lawyer, who is not going to be me."

"Thanks a lot."

"Don't talk to me, McKenna. I mean it. Don't talk to me and don't talk to Martinez and don't talk to the judge when we get to court, because whether you know it or not, you're going to be arraigned tonight."

I opened my eyes. "The man from the district attorney's office," I said.

"Exactly."

I looked up the stairs to where the little army of men was stationed. There seemed to be hundreds of them—many more than had been in my apartment. There were men with little black bags and men with cameras and a policewoman with a face Medusa would have died for. I wondered where they'd found her. The policewomen I saw on the streets were all pretty, young, attractive women.

"What's an arraignment, anyway?" I asked Nick.

He sniffed at me. "An arraignment is where they ask you if you're guilty or not guilty."

"For God's sake," I said. "I haven't even been arrested."

"Give it time."

I looked away, back at the army of men. I thought about my father and my mother and my brother in Connecticut. I was going to have to tell them something eventually. What? That I kept stumbling over bodies the way other people tripped on the subway stairs? That everything would be all right and I'd come out of this with the fattest crime book contract in the history of publishing? That at the moment being handed over to an institution for the criminally insane would be good luck?

It would have been better if Nick had maintained his earlier sympathy. I wanted him to hold my hand. He was sitting with his arms folded across his chest, hands under elbows.

A door slammed open. Martinez came in on little cat feet—or elephant hooves, take your pick.

"Miss McKenna," Martinez said, "Miss McKenna, I would most sincerely like to talk to you."

He sounded anything but sincere, but I got to my feet anyway. Nick got up with me. He brushed the lint off his pants and examined his fingernails (dirty) at the same time.

"I take it you're her lawyer," Martinez said.

"For the present," Nick said.

"I used to know somebody else traveled with their lawyer. Bonanno family, I think."

"Lieutenant—"

"Never mind," Martinez said, turning on his heel.

The police had taken over one of the conference rooms, a gaudy gold-leaf and red velveteen monument to bland pretentiousness that held one fake mahogany table, eighteen captain's chairs, a blackboard, and a draw-down map of Texas. Nick and I sat across from each other at one end of the table. Martinez sat near us at the head, like a Victorian paterfamilias.

"Should I read her her rights?" Martinez said.

"Are you arresting my client?"

"Somebody's arresting your client," Martinez said. "Mr. McReady—"

The little man from the DA's office bustled in, admirably on cue. His tie was twisted over his shoulder and the hair he had left hung limp with sweat against the pitted scars on his cheeks. He hurried to the far end of the table and sat down, divorcing himself from the proceedings.

"Now," Martinez said, looking straight at me. "Do you have *any* explanation for this thing? Anything at all?"

"Don't answer that," Nick said.

"This whole thing is a huge misunderstanding," I said.

"Oh, for God's sake," Nick said.

"A body locked in your apartment is not a misunderstanding," Martinez said. "A second body you just happen to stumble over is not a misunderstanding."

"You're assuming things," I said. "You're assuming Myrra wasn't murdered by a mugger. If Myrra was murdered by a mugger, you don't have *one shred of motive*—"

"Shut up," Nick shouted. "If you don't want my advice, you don't have to take it, but you don't have to have me here representing you, either. If you want me here representing you, you will sit down, shut up, and answer only those questions I tell you to answer."

I folded my arms across my chest. Martinez sighed.

"The bag," he said. "I would like to see what's in the bag. Can she do that, Mr. Carras—"

Nick hesitated.

"Oh, for God's sake," I said. I upended the bag on the table, letting my life spill out, cat and all. Martinez stared at the debris.

"What is all this stuff?" he asked. "Three wallets? Why do you need three wallets?"

"One of them's Phoebe's," I said. I picked up a brown suede one and looked inside. "This one's Hazel Ganz's."

"You tell me," Martinez said. "What are you doing with Miss Damereaux's wallet? And Miss—"

"Hazel Ganz," I said. "She steals things."

"Hazel Ganz steals things."

"No," I said. "The cat." I gestured to Camille, who had the corner of Martinez's ID folder in her mouth and was dutifully dragging it across the table toward the tote bag. "I put the tote bag down in the ladies' room when we were all there, and I suppose—"

Martinez retrieved his ID from Camille. "A kleptomaniac cat," he said. "I don't think I want to know anything about a kleptomaniac cat." He waved his hand over the rest of the pile. "What else?"

Nick coughed. "I think that's enough of this, Lieutenant," he said. "Perhaps you would let my client clean up this mess and return—"

"She's not going to return anything," Martinez said. "How the hell do I know what's going to be important?"

"What do you think is going to be important?" Nick said. "This? It's a corkscrew. This? As far as I can tell, it's a lipstick. What about the penlight? There isn't blood on any of this stuff."

He stood there waving the penlight in his hands, right under Martinez's nose. I reached into my pocket and found my cigarettes, trying to keep my hands from shaking. We'd been looking for days, we'd been driving each other crazy, and the solution had been here all the time. The only possible solution. The only sensible solution.

Nick was standing a few feet away from me, holding the penlight like a magic wand. I was sure that at any minute Nick would flick the switch and let Martinez know what I already knew.

He didn't get a chance. Martinez stood up and waved around something of his own. The warrant.

"Patience Campbell McKenna," Martinez said, "I hereby arrest you—"

I reached across the table and started shoving things into my tote bag, beginning with the penlight.

Because, of course, it wasn't a penlight at all.

It was a *magnet.*

CHAPTER 31

The policewoman with Medusa's face loved the cat. She held Camille in her lap and petted her all the time I was being booked, finger-printed, folded, spindled, and mutilated. She made cooing noises in Camille's ears. Camille, who began by preening and purring, ended by taking a bite out of the woman's right thumb.

I answered a lot of silly questions about my next of kin and marital status. I thought about that magnet. I thought about it until my head felt ready to crack open, but I still couldn't make it all come together.

I now knew how somebody had locked Julie Simms's body in my apartment. Knowing how, I also knew who. Unfortunately, there was no conceivable motive whatsoever for that person to have killed not one but three of her acquaintances. Acquaintances, not even friends.

Something was wrong at Fires of Love, I told myself stubbornly. What could go wrong that any one of the people on Myrra's list could have caused? Every time I tried to find an answer, I came up with: nothing. I knew what it couldn't be. It couldn't be Farret cheating on royalty statements or foreign rights sales, because Amelia and Phoebe and Julie could not have been responsible for those crimes. It couldn't have been a plagiarism scandal either. In that case, either one of the writers or Farret would have to be involved, and both of them could be. Marty Caine, however, could not be. There might be a conspiracy, but I didn't believe it. And what about Julie? What could an agent do that a writer, an editor, and a marketing director could also do, at least in the way of business crime? Nothing, nothing, nothing.

Nothing left me sitting at Central Booking, explaining to an embar-rassed adolescent in a blue uniform that I did not now have any serious communicable diseases, had never had any serious communicable diseases, and never intended to have any serious communicable diseases. He nodded without looking at me and went on to "physical impediments."

Nick stood at the phone normally reserved for prisoners making their one call and fed dimes into it while he half shouted and half whispered a very complicated set of instructions to his law partner. He came back about the time the adolescent got to "necessary prescribed medication."

"We got it," Nick said. "Phoebe got her banker out of bed."

"You don't know if I'm going to get bail."

Nick glared at the adolescent, who made blushing apologies, grabbed his papers, and hurried away. It was a frail victory, but the only one available.

"I can't believe you," Nick said to me. "Keys. Knives. *Wallets.* For God's sake, haven't you been telling me anything?"

"You know the penlight?" I asked him. "It's not a penlight. It's a magnet."

"What's that supposed to mean?"

"I'm trying to tell you everything," I said. "The penlight that fell out of my tote bag isn't a penlight. It's a magnet. A very small electric magnet. With batteries."

"So what?"

"So that's how somebody locked Julie Simms in my apartment." He looked interested. He looked so interested, I got careless. "I know who killed Myrra," I told him. "I don't know how to prove it, but at least—"

He was already on his feet and walking away from me.

I slumped in my chair. The arraignment court in Manhattan runs twenty-four hours a day. I could be arraigned for murder, even jailed without bail, at any moment. And Nick wouldn't listen to me.

I went over to the desk where the uniformed adolescent was still working on my forms.

"Do I still get one phone call?" I asked him.

"What?"

"Do I still get one phone call? You know, my lawyer's here, but he came with me, I didn't call him. So—"

"Oh," the adolescent said. "Yeah. Sure. Go right ahead."

I borrowed the dime from a black man with a ruby in his ear and the scent of jasmine in his hair. Then I waited ten minutes behind a prostitute in hip-high leg warmers and a red stocking cap. When I finally got through to Phoebe, she sounded drunk.

"Everybody's here," she shouted over the background din. "Janine, Amelia, Lydia, even Hazel Ganz. Everybody. We're planning strategy."

I knew better than to ask her what that meant. I told her to get on the phone in the bedroom, lock the door, and not let anyone in. It took a little time, but I finally heard her voice coming through silence.

"Where are you?" she said. "Have they let you out?"

"I'm at Central Booking. They aren't going to let me out, at least not tonight. Listen, Phoebe, I don't have a lot of time. Just tell me *what* the Fires of Love Advisory Board did."

"What?"

I sighed. "Phoebe, I don't want to explain things, I just want to know what the Fires of Love Advisory Board did. Give speeches? Go on public relations tours?"

"Are you crazy?" Phoebe was chirping. It was always a bad sign when Phoebe chirped. "You're being arrested for murder, for God's sake. What do you care about the Advisory Board? Are you on drugs? Are they beating you?"

"Phoebe."

"All right." She paused. I thought I heard the sound of champagne being swallowed. "You're perfectly serious?"

"Phoebe, for God's sake, I've only got three minutes on this phone."

"Right." Another pause. More swallowed champagne. I promised myself I'd break a bottle of it over her head the next time I saw her.

"We made up the tip sheet," Phoebe said finally, "except that didn't matter because Janine changed it. We did a lot of interviews, talked to *Romantic Times*, that kind of thing. We each wrote a book for the line, maybe two, and then there were reader parties and the bookstores drives and—"

"Back up," I said. "What's a bookstore drive?"

"It was to get the bookstores selling Farret romances again. They didn't really want to after Romantic Life failed. Readers would talk their bookstores into having a party for one of us, and we'd go out there and hawk books, and then if everything went right, the bookstore started stocking Fires of Love. Sometimes you'd go out to do one and the fans would have a couple more lined up. Omaha. Places like that."

I hung on the phone and tried to think. "What happened if you got to Omaha for one bookstore and found you had six?"

"Well, you always had lots of books," Phoebe said. "I'll give that to Marty Caine. I went out to Cleveland, I was met by two thousand copies. Unbelievable. If you had extra bookstores you took the books and these little computer cards, like the cards to register in college, you know? And you wrote all the information about the extra store on the card and the number of books sold, and then Marty got in touch with them."

"Hot damn," I said.

"What?" Phoebe said.

"I gotta use that phone," somebody behind me said.

There was a sound of splintering wood. I dropped the receiver and spun around.

If I hadn't been so tired, I might have tried to hide under the wooden bench next to the phone. I might even have become hysterical.

Instead, I was as calm as if I was watching that scene in a movie.

The black man with the ruby in his ear was taking the place apart. He had kicked through the rail between the desk area and reception. He was making hamburger out of some officer's desk. About fifty police officers were crowded around him, waving handcuffs in the air. More were coming. None of them were looking at me.

One of them had left the door open.

I decided I didn't know what I was waiting for.

CHAPTER 32

It wasn't the most ingenious escape in the history of New York City crime. I didn't hide in heating ducts, disguise myself as a bar of soap, or run through the sewer tunnels. I did what any good New Yorker— especially a resident of Manhattan—would do. I walked out the front of the building and caught a cab.

I was more careful when I got to the Cathay-Pierce. I didn't want Myrra Agenworth's murderer to see me. I went in a side entrance and up the service elevator.

I knew who had done it, why it had been done, and what I needed to prove it. All I needed was to get my hands on two pieces of paper. I already had one of them.

Phoebe was asleep on the couch when I got up to the suite. I tiptoed past her into the bedroom, exchanged evening pajamas for jeans and sweater, and tiptoed out again. She took one look at me and screamed.

"For God's sake," she said. "Why didn't you call? Why didn't you wake me up?"

The phone rang. I put my hand over hers.

"I'm not here. No matter who it is, no matter what they want, I'm not here."

She gave me a suspicious look, picked up the phone, and winced. I didn't blame her. They could have heard Nick in New Jersey.

He wasn't asking for information, he was giving it.

"I will remain that woman's counsel," he shouted, "just as long as it takes me to catch up with her and strangle her. Do you hear me, Weiss? *Strangle* her."

Phoebe kneaded her forehead. I lit a cigarette. Nick said something about being on the way over and hung up.

"You broke out of jail," she said. "I can't believe it."

"I didn't break out of jail," I said. "I walked out. The door was wide open." I took a deep drag. "Nick won't help me," I said. "You've got to. I know who did it, I know why, and I think I can prove it. Only we've got to get hold of this stuff *now.*"

"I'm listening."

I told her the whole story. I told her everything I had figured out in the cab, and threw in a few suppositions to make it sound better. When I got to the part about how the scam worked, I went very, very carefully.

"It was those bookstore parties," I told her. "That's what confused Myrra. You all went out on those bookstore parties. You all had access to those computer cards. Any one of you could have been making out five or six extra cards every trip, saying you sold hundreds of extra books—"

"But someone would catch it," Phoebe said. "Someone would notice no money was coming in, or no extra books going out—"

"Of course they would," I said. "In about a year. When an overall accounting was done. Maybe. In the meantime, when do you think was the last time the comptroller of Farret talked to one of the editors?"

Phoebe grimaced. "They're not even in the same building."

"Any one of you could have hyped Fires of Love figures for any book you wanted to. Any one of you could have had a reason. The writers might want to make their sales look better or make more money from royalties. Same with Julie—the better a writer's sales, the better the advance on the next book, the better the percentage Julie picks up. Janine and Marty had a stake in the overall success of the line—"

"But you're talking about a huge hype," Phoebe said.

"I know." I lit another cigarette. It was getting late. We had to hurry, but I couldn't tell this any faster and make sense.

"Everybody kept telling us," I said. "Everybody kept repeating it over and over and over again. We should have known all along. Myrra knew from the beginning."

"That Fires of Love wasn't having a hundred-million-dollar year."

"Not even close," I said. "I think she knew who was doing it by June at the latest. I don't know why she kept the blackmail files on all of you going—leverage, I guess, in case she couldn't prove what she needed to. Then in October the reports came. Myrra got a royalty report and a general report on the line. You probably got one yourself. They were probably sent to all the Advisory Board members. I've seen a couple of them floating around here this weekend."

"Inflated reports," Phoebe said.

"No," I said. "Perfectly honest reports. That's how Myrra knew who was doing it. Our murderer didn't need to lie to the general public, you see. Our murderer needed to lie only to a very select group of people, two or three at the most."

"And Myrra wasn't one of them." Phoebe's face was pinched.

"Our murderer didn't think so. Only the people who had to got those inflated reports. Everybody else got a perfectly honest accounting. Only two people were in a position to pull that off. Only one of them had to."

"You're out of your mind." The skin under Phoebe's eyes was pulled taut. Shock warred with anger—anger against our murderer. Some of my own tension began to dissolve. If Phoebe was angry this way, she would be on my side.

Still, she needed to be convinced.

"Do you realize what you're talking about?" she asked me. "Three murders. You're trying to tell me that a perfectly sane human being committed three murders—"

"It had to be done," I said gently. "It could have been just Myrra if it wasn't for the conference, for the line award. If Farret was going to win the line award, more people were going to have to be taken into the lie—"

"You don't know any of this for true," she said.

"All we have to do is go down there and check," I said.

Outside, it was very dark and very clear and very wet. In the fifth floor hall, it was just deserted. There is something about the hallways of hotels at night. Doors open just as you turn your back. Creatures follow you, their steps swallowed by thick carpets. The executioner is just over your shoulder. He will disappear if you look.

Phoebe padded along, oblivious. When she looked over her shoulder, it was to frown at me.

"You have to hurry."

I hurried. The door, when we got to it, was like any other door. The numbers were carved in the wood at what was supposed to be eye level. Eye level for a midget, I thought, rattling the knob.

"Someone might already be here," I said.

"Then they'll be caught in the act," Phoebe said. "That much better."

"You wouldn't be so calm if you believed me."

When she didn't answer, I rattled the knob again. Then I borrowed one of her hairpins and leaned down beside the keyhole, cursing the passion for verisimilitude that prevented the Cathay-Pierce from installing the kind of locks that could be opened with credit cards.

I felt something give and followed it around as far as I could. It was only the first minor success, but at least it was progress. I tried to think of something to do in case I couldn't get into that room, or if what we wanted wasn't there. Copies. Who had which copies? Whose copies mattered?

The Line Committee had to have been given the falsified copies. These were the copies I needed to find. I was assuming they had been returned to Farret and therefore to this suite. I could be wrong. Phoebe and I both could be proceeding out of nothing that even resembled a fact.

I might even be wrong about everything.

I tugged at the lock, jiggled the hairpin, tugged again. I spent five minutes going backward. I was sure I had locked something I had unlocked, then unlocked it again.

"For God's sake," Phoebe said. "They have to have guards in this hotel. Nick is probably already here."

She pushed me aside, stuck another hairpin in the door, and shook it twice. The doorknob jiggled under her hand. I stared at it in a stupor.

You were not supposed to be able to open doors with hairpins. You certainly weren't supposed to do it on the first try.

"Come on," Phoebe said. "We're going to get caught."

I followed her in and shut the door behind us. My hand went automatically to the light switch and then stopped. I looked at the night lights of Manhattan from the window of the street.

"We can't turn anything on," I said. "Somebody might see the lights from the hall."

"I can't see my hand in front of my face," Phoebe said.

"Shhh." I tried to listen, sure I had heard a sound from somewhere else in the suite. I heard nothing. I grabbed Phoebe by the wrist and pulled her along. What we were looking for wouldn't be in the main room, I told myself. There wouldn't be anything here but book displays and tip sheets.

I bumped into a table, fell, and let go of Phoebe's wrist. Somewhere in the darkness, I heard the door of the bedroom sliding open.

"Who is it?" I said. "Where are you?" I tried to get up, but the pain in my knee was unbearable. I started dragging myself along the carpet, trying to get out of the way, against the wall and in the darkness. I heard door hinges creak. I heard bare feet rubbing against carpet.

"Phoebe?" I said. I knew I shouldn't have said anything. I shouldn't have moved. I should have sat still where I was and tried not to breathe. I couldn't do it. I felt as if I was in the middle of a ghost story, complete with wailing spirits and rattling chains.

I kept thinking about doors in hallways. No one was watching the hallways. Creatures were escaping from the doors, parading down the stairs into the ballrooms.

If class is grace under pressure, I have little of it. I crouched, frozen, against my small section of wall, listening to footsteps on the carpet and feeling my mind disintegrate. People were walking around in the center of the room, looking for me, watching for me, and I couldn't tell where they were. Phoebe and someone else. I couldn't concentrate.

I wanted nothing more than to scream.

There was a brush of air and a low moaning sound almost like laughter. I said, "Phoebe," without thinking. Someone said, "No."

No. I heard it and didn't comprehend it. I had gone stiffer than a rabbit stopped in a road by the headlights of a car. Above my head, the blade of a knife glinted in the lights from the streetlamps.

So did something else, round and brass-gold.

At which point Phoebe smashed the base of a four-foot-high china table lamp over Janine Williams's head.

EPILOGUE

On the evening of the day Sotheby Parke Bernet took delivery of Myrra's furniture, Daniel called. He called my old apartment and was directed to Myrra's. When the phone rang, I was standing in the kitchen, barren without its refectory table, trying to determine one level tablespoon of sugar by the light of a bayberry candle. Phoebe was right. I should have made them leave at least one lamp.

"Listen," Daniel said. "I just wanted to see how you were doing."

I gave up trying to measure. I dumped sugar into milk with a liberal hand. Chocolate fondue is supposed to be sweet.

"We ought to get together," Daniel said. "We haven't had a night out in a long time."

"Ten days," I said. "Ever since Julie Simms was murdered in my apartment."

Daniel coughed. I could hear Phoebe and Nick in the living room. It sounded like they were popping balloons with candles. Considering what those balloons cost me (you have to replace furniture with something), I was going to kill them.

"You know," Daniel said. "The tree's lit in Rockefeller Center. You always said—"

"How did the partnership work out? Did you get it?"

"Now Patience," Daniel said. "After three years—"

I hung up.

Phoebe and Nick were stretched out on the floor of what looked, without furniture, like the Grand Ballroom of the old Waldorf. Phoebe had made a circle on the carpet with hemming chalk, and they were pitching pennies.

I considered what I knew about Nick: He was taller than I was. He was good to his mother. He kept his socks in the refrigerator

I put the chocolate fondue on the floor on a potholder.

"Now," I said. "Back to the point. It was perfectly simple—"

Nick groaned. "If it was perfectly simple, you wouldn't have Martinez on the verge of suicide."

"But it was," I said. "It was perfectly simple." I reached for the papers I had been writing on during dinner. "Look. What did we all know about Fires of Love?"

"It had a hundred-million-dollar year."

"And nobody could understand why," I said. "Amelia kept saying it didn't make sense, and I didn't listen to her. In fact, almost nobody liked that line. Even Hazel Ganz voted against every Fires of Love book at the First Novel meeting, and she *writes* for Fires of Love."

"So?" Nick said. "I thought publishing people were notorious for not knowing a good thing when they saw it."

"Sure they are," I said. "But in this case, it wasn't an editor in some obscure publishing company saying something wouldn't work. It was Amelia Samson, who doesn't know much about writing, but does know more about marketing than Burger King and McDonald's put together. And she was right. Fires of Love didn't do one thing some other line didn't do better. And that in a field well beyond the saturation point when Fires of Love *started*.

"Now look at this. Romantic Life, Farret's last line before Fires of Love did so badly the brass was threatening to fire everybody and shut down romance operations altogether. Fires of Love didn't do too well the first month it was out, either. Then all of a sudden, it turned into a smash. And Myrra got suspicious.

"The thing is, she had to have seen those figures at the beginning of April. She'd see the advances. She was on that Advisory Board. I think in the beginning she thought it was just Amelia or Lydia or even Phoebe hyping the bookstore sales. Go out to Omaha, as Phoebe put it, and instead of saying you sold at one bookstore, say you sold at three. Make out a couple of extra cards, pay the difference for a couple of hundred books yourself. Phoebe and Lydia and Amelia could have done it financially. So could Julie."

"But why would anyone want to?" Nick complained.

"Everybody had a reason," Phoebe said quickly. "I might have needed my first category to be a success, because all my other books are successes, and I wouldn't want to look a failure. Amelia's been slipping in sales for a while. She can't get used to the sex scenes. Lydia's been slipping, too. There isn't as much call for bodice rippers as there used to be."

"And Julie had clients to protect," I went on. "When you get to Janine and Marty Caine, things get a little more sinister. Then it has to be major fraud.

"And it was, but not of the kind you'd expect. Janine wasn't trying to make money, she was just trying to keep her job. She'd already been responsible for the biggest, most expensive failure in publishing. Her only options were to make a success out of Fires of Love or leave Farret. And she'd never get as good a position again.

"So. What she did was to fix the computer system. When you punched in a code for Myrra or Julie or Phoebe, you got a perfectly accurate report on books sold where, when, and how. When you punched executive office code, or Janine's personal code, or Marty's, you got the inflated figures. The head of the accounting department got inflated figures, with money shaved from other divisions. The peon in the contracts office who made out the checks and the middle management flunky who had to okay them got accurate figures. If you didn't know what you were looking for, it would have taken years to figure it out. I figured most of it out and Marty Caine had to explain it to me."

"Did Marty Caine figure it out beforehand?" Phoebe asked. "He didn't seem—surprised."

"I don't think he was," I said. "He kept giving us hints, too, you know. He kept telling us there were problems. And he kept telling us Janine knew how to handle the problems. But Marty Caine wasn't a danger to Janine. He had the same problems she did.

"Myrra, on the other hand, was a real disaster. As soon as she smelled something wrong, she started digging. And digging. And digging. And when Myrra started digging, she found things. I think Janine must have realized there wasn't much time."

"How did she get that old woman out to Riverside Park at two-thirty in the morning?" Nick asked.

"She called up and said she was Pay," Phoebe said. "She did the same thing to me, the night Leslie Ashe was stabbed. She probably said she was Pay and in trouble and please bring the keys, and Myrra—"

"Those *keys*." Nick sounded as if he was being stabbed himself. "The keys that weren't supposed to exist. You could have told Martinez about those keys in the first place, you know. It would have saved me two days at the 20th Precinct."

"It didn't seem important at the time," I said. "And besides, Janine didn't take the keys to get into my apartment, she took them to get into Myrra's apartment." I looked around the room. "This apartment. You know what I mean. Anyway, Janine being Janine being Janine, and not wanting to get caught too soon, took Esmeralda to the pound. That kept the dog from going right back to Myrra's apartment and alarming the doorman. She kept most of Myrra's jewelry, but she left one earring on Esmeralda's collar. I don't think she knew what to do with the necklace, so she sent it to the Jewels of Love Committee.

"Now, the afternoon of Myrra's funeral, Julie walked up to her and said Hazel Ganz was complaining her book wasn't making enough money. Janine freaked. She hadn't been able to get into Myrra's apartment. Julie was one of the few people on earth who would be able to tell what was going wrong with the executive reports. The last thing Janine wanted was to have Julie go over Hazel's statements item by item, then sit on the Line Committee and go over those executive reports. And Janine had to submit those executive reports to the committee. She needed them to counterbalance the reports of the booksellers, which were largely negative.

"Janine either called Julie and said she was me, or said she was herself and speaking for me, and asked Julie to come to my apartment. She probably said she was me, because she'd want to cover herself. And it had to be my apartment, because she wanted to link Myrra and Julie, if she had to. She didn't expect Myrra to leave me the apartment. She thought someone might have overheard her call on the night of Myrra's death.

"Anyway, she used Myrra's keys to get into my apartment. Julie came in, she stabbed her, put Myrra's earring in her purse, then turned off all the lights and locked up. Then she used that penlight thing and drew the bolt from the outside. It wasn't hard to do, you know. It's not a very strong electric magnet, but my bolt is nothing more than one of those little notched things. And I tried it this afternoon—"

"On the guest bathroom," Phoebe sighed. "We got it locked. We just couldn't get it open again."

"You know, Marty suspected that part, too. That penlight thing is part of a game the marketing guys have set up in the hall at Farret. They make discs move like flying saucers. And they're right out in the hall across from Janine's office. I saw them playing it the day after Julie's murder.

"Anyway, the bolt kept Barbara from coming in and finding the body, which kept me from having an alibi, which is what Janine wanted. I think I'm going to give up telling Barbara stories in public. At any rate, I was too fast. I got Carlos and had the place broken into right away. The times were wrong.

"In the meantime, however, Janine was covering herself. She took the knife, which she didn't need any longer—or she thought she didn't—and brought it over to Julie's apartment building sometime early on the morning after the second murder. Jaimie Hallman found it there the next morning. He was afraid he'd be suspected, so he started trying to give it to me. He figured—I don't know what he figured. But the police certainly didn't want to listen to him.

"Now, on Saturday, Janine got a shock. She knew Mary Allard smelled a fish in the whole Fires of Love operation, but she wasn't worried about it. Mary Allard talked to booksellers. She kept a close eye on her line and everyone else's. But nobody ever listened to her. Ever since that audit, she'd been a pariah.

"Then Mary Allard turned up with a letter from Julie asking to put her on the Line Committee. I think Julie knew a lot more than she was letting on, you know. That business about 'if anything happens to me' makes me squirm.

"Now Janine really had a problem. Mary wanted nothing more than to catch one of what she called the 'pink and greens' in something dishonest. And she had to know Fires of Love wasn't doing as well as Janine said it was. Janine had Leslie Ashe, too. Leslie was hauling around a copy of Myrra's royalty reports, trying to find a way to get a look at those printouts.

"Saturday night Leslie asked to go up to the suite and get copies of some of Myrra's books. Janine called Phoebe, said she was me, and made an appointment to meet at the Farret hospitality suite at six-thirty. When Leslie left the table, Janine took a hotel kitchen knife, followed her, waited till she got in the door on five, and then started stabbing. She didn't have a lot of time, and she didn't do a very good job. It didn't matter. She didn't need to kill Leslie, anyway, just deflect her until after the conference.

"She did have to kill Mary, however. And she had to implicate me thoroughly. You know, all that Sunday, every time I saw Janine, something else turned up in my tote bag. The keys. The real murder *knife.*"

"How did she get the knife back?" Nick said. "I thought Jaimie Hallman had it and lost it."

"She stole it from him in the elevator when he was coming to Phoebe's suite. It was a nice touch, but it didn't matter. She could have used any knife.

"Anyway, she kept dropping things in my bag. She dropped the knife in there during the preliminaries at the reception. Camille hated it. She hated it. I had to take her out of there and put her in my pocket. I thought it was just that Janine had bumped into me and upset the cat. I didn't find the knife until later.

"I found the knife while I was trying to sober Phoebe up. I took it out of my bag and put it on the couch. Janine found it on the couch and took it back.

"Then she really did something smart. She didn't ask Mary to meet her. She took a wad of computer printouts from her purse—not the

Sweet, Savage Death

real ones, mind you—and pretended to be trying to get rid of it. Mary followed her. Of course Mary followed her."

"Across the stage," Phoebe said.

"Exactly. I saw Mary. I took off after Mary. Janine heard the commotion and started to run. Mary took off after Janine. I don't know how Janine got Mary up the staircase, but she did. I got to the staircase half a minute after Janine escaped."

"And this is supposed to be simple," Nick said. "You give me a headache."

I looked at the light and shadow cast by the candles. I would have to do something about furniture. I would have to do it soon. Myrra's furniture would be sold to set up a trust to pay the maintenance fees on the apartment—probably until the year 3000—but in the meantime I could afford a little Danish modern. Or Upper West Side antique. At least a bed.

"Where's Camille?" I yawned.

"In the fondue," Phoebe said.

I looked into the fondue pot. A furry black head ducked just below the rim, licking paws covered with chocolate.

"Damn," I said. "This morning she was trying to sit in a can of tuna fish. I must have given her a complex."

"You'll have to get her out of there and clean her up," Phoebe said.

"She'll clean herself up," Nick said. "Somebody open another bottle of wine."

I passed him the wine and told him to open it himself. I was thinking about Myrra's apartment, now mine, with its six walk-in closets and full pantry and overhead storage spaces. That place rattled in the night. Things moved.

I took the wine from Nick and opened it myself. Maybe, if I could get them drunk enough, they would agree to camp out with me for the night.